THE
Mitzvah Project
BOOK
Making Part of Your bar/bat mitzvah … and Your Life

Liz Suneby & Diane Heiman

Foreword by Rabbi Jeffrey K. Salkin
Preface by Rabbi Sharon Brous
Illustrations by Laurel Molk

For People of All Faiths, All Backgrounds

JEWISH LIGHTS Publishing
Woodstock, Vermont

The Mitzvah Project Book:
Making Mitzvah Part of Your Bar/Bat Mitzvah ... and Your Life

2011 Quality Paperback Edition, First Printing
© 2011 by Liz Suneby and Diane Heiman
Foreword © by Jeffrey K. Salkin
Preface © by Rabbi Sharon Brous

Library of Congress Cataloging-in-Publication Data
Suneby, Elizabeth, 1958–
  The mitzvah project book : making mitzvah part of your bar/bat mitzvah ... and your life / Elizabeth Suneby & Diane Heiman ; foreword by Jeffrey K. Salkin ; preface by Sharon Brous ; Illustrations by Laurel Molk.
  p. cm.
Includes bibliographical references.
ISBN 978-1-58023-458-0 (quality pbk. original) 1. Bar mitzvah—Handbooks, manuals, etc.—Juvenile literature. 2. Bat mitzvah—Handbooks, manuals, etc.—Juvenile literature. 3. Jewish way of life—Juvenile literature. I. Heiman, Diane. II. Title.
BM707.2.S86 2011
296.4'424—dc23
2011021304

10 9 8 7 6 5 4 3 2 1

Manufactured in the United States of America

Cover and Interior Design: Heather Pelham
Cover Art: Laurel Molk

For People of All Faiths, All Backgrounds
Published by Jewish Lights Publishing
A Division of LongHill Partners, Inc.
Sunset Farm Offices, Route 4, P.O. Box 237
Woodstock, VT 05091
Tel: (802) 457-4000   Fax: (802) 457-4004
www.jewishlights.com

For all the young people who shared their mitzvah
projects with us and for my father,
Sidney S. Barzman,
who leads by example with kindness,
integrity, and optimism. —DH

For Josh, my old soul; Emma, my muse; and Per,
my biggest supporter. —LS

Contents

Mitzvah Project Ideas
Real Kids, Real Mitzvot Stories & Journal Pages

Foreword

Rabbi Jeffrey K. Salkin

This Note Is for You—the Kid Who Is Becoming Bar or Bat Mitzvah

I can only imagine that sometimes this whole thing feels rather scary—learning Hebrew; learning the Torah and haftarah portion; perhaps learning how to chant it all; and most likely, writing a *d'var Torah* (sermonette). You may even be saying to yourself: "OK, I'm going through this 'event' in my life, and, sure, I'm going to be great. But really—two days or two weeks or two years after it's over, what difference will it have made to anyone besides me and my loved ones?"

That's probably the best reason I know for you to do a mitzvah project. It guarantees that even and especially after the ceremony and the festivities are over, and even and especially after you've completed your thank-you notes, your becoming Bar or Bat Mitzvah will *mean something*. And that's one of the most important reasons I wrote *For Kids—Putting God on Your Guest List: How to Claim the Spiritual Meaning of Your Bar or Bat Mitzvah* (Jewish Lights) for you. It means that in some small way, you did something that changed someone's life. In some small way, you repaired a broken piece of the world and made it whole.

I imagine what you might be thinking: "It's not like I am going to cure AIDS or reverse global warming or end famine in Africa. Who am I, Bono?" True, those tasks are way beyond any *one* person's ability (even Bono and every other celebrity who wants to make a difference).

But, as our tradition says, "It's not up to you to complete the task. But neither are you allowed to try to get out of even starting it" (*Pirke Avot* 2:16). Thank you, really, for devoting your energies to making the world just a little bit better. By doing so, you are saying to yourself, and to others, that this whole Bar/Bat Mitzvah thing is real and important. And, this book will help you figure out great ways to put your own passions, interests, and hobbies to work for mitzvah.

This Is a Note for Your Parents, Rabbi, Cantor, Teacher, and Other Adults in Your Life

When my brother called to tell me that the old Huntington Town House on the north shore of Long Island had gone out of business and was being converted into a Best Buy, I knew that it was the end of an era. The Huntington Town House was the default Saturday afternoon address of my young adolescence, the overdone and garish location of countless over-the-top Bar Mitzvah celebrations of the 1960s and early 1970s. (I say "Bar" Mitzvah and not "Bat" Mitzvah deliberately; there were, alas, very few in those days.) I can honestly say that spending countless Saturday afternoons in poorly lit party spaces took its toll on our young lives. My peers and I emerged from those experiences not only seriously deprived of quality outdoor time, but also somewhat jaded about the whole enterprise.

It's all American Jewish folklore: the themes, the candlelighting ceremonies, the T-shirts that proclaim you attended Brian's Bar Mitzvah—not to mention the sheer expenditure of money....

But, as Bob Dylan (who turns seventy years old as I write this) famously sang, "The times, they are a-changing." The quiet revolution in Jewish celebration started more than thirty years ago, with the creation of MAZON, A Jewish Response to Hunger, which asked families to give 3 percent of the cost of a *simcha* (celebration) to fighting world hunger. And then, many Jewish families started to "twin" with Soviet Jewish children.

As I encourage in *Putting God on the Guest List: How to Reclaim the Spiritual Meaning of Your Child's Bar or Bat Mitzvah* (Jewish Lights), Jewish families have begun to quietly yet firmly reject the culture of glitz that has often surrounded Bar/Bat Mitzvah. Instead, they want a different kind of celebration. They are no longer interested in their celebration being *impressive*; they want it to be *expressive* of core Jewish values like *mitzvah, tzedakah* (charity), and *tikkun olam* (repairing the world).

For that reason alone, we should be grateful to Liz Suneby and Diane Heiman for this book. They have done an admirable job of coming up with ideas for mitzvah projects for Bar/Bat Mitzvah. And they have done so in a very enticing way. Their tone is conversational and personal, and they are adept at helping young people put their strengths to work for mitzvah.

Not only this: Liz and Diane subtly address one of the biggest challenges in all of our contemporary mitzvah work. They focus on the balance between particularism (what we do for the Jewish people) and universalism (what we do for others). They see no dichotomy; it's all in there, from helping people in your community to helping Israel. That's exactly how it should be: "If I am not for myself, who will be for me? But if I am only for myself, what am I?" (*Pirke Avot* 1:14).

I am personally and professionally grateful for this book, because when I start scratching my head, trying to come up with ideas for mitzvah projects for my students, it will be on my shelf and it will serve as a ready resource. Linguists say that every two weeks, a language becomes extinct. Liz and Diane have made sure that the native Jewish language of mitzvah and compassion will never become extinct.

Preface

Rabbi Sharon Brous

"So what was your Bar Mitzvah theme?" I asked.

"I don't understand," he replied.

"You know, your theme. Superheroes. The tropics. Cirque d'Soliel. Cavemen. Mine was ice cream. Every table a different flavor," I said.

After a stupefied silence he replied, "The theme of my Bar Mitzvah was Torah."

This is the first conversation I remember having with the cute red-head across the hall in my first-year dorm in college. Years later we got married, and he still occasionally ribs me about it. The Judaism I knew—embodied in my Bat Mitzvah experience—was about memorization, recitation, and ostentation, not learning, spiritual growth, and dedication. It took me years to realize that the real gift of the Bat Mitzvah was not the mountains of freshwater pearls, Israel bonds, or the themed party, but the voice, the vision, and the real responsibility that comes with being a Jew who engages deeply with Torah.

A Bar or Bat Mitzvah experience built around serious engagement with Torah necessarily cultivates and communicates a sense of responsibility. The goal is not to *have* a Bar or Bat Mitzvah, but to *become* a Bar or Bat Mitzvah. Your task is to learn deeply and emerge awake both to the brokenness of the world and to your responsibility to work toward its transformation.

Consider the midrash that tells of a traveler who notices a *birah doleket*—a palace consumed in flames. He is stunned by the sight and wonders: "How can it be that nobody is taking care of this palace—that it is left to burn? Who is responsible for this place?"

At that moment, the owner of the palace hears him and says, "I am the owner of this place!"

So, too, the midrash teaches, Abraham wonders, "Is it possible that the world should just burn without someone working to save it? Who is responsible for this place?"

And the Holy One hears him and says, "I am the owner of this world!" (Genesis Rabbah 39:1).

The Rabbis wonder what it is about Abraham that he merits being the first Jew. Here they posit: despite his luxurious life and bountiful blessings, he is able to look up and see that the world is on fire. But he does not merely make this observation. He is certain that *someone* must be responsible, so he demands to know who it is. He calls the owner to step forward: "What are You doing about it?" And the owner responds, "What are *you* doing about it?" Together, they go to put out the fire.

From Torah we learn that Judaism is born in the wakeful resistance to the status quo. As God's covenantal partner, we are taught to bristle at the injustices of the world. The Jew is called to hear the cry of the oppressed, to witness the pain of the afflicted, to agonize over the plight of the poor. Torah teaches that as Jews we stand in the chasm between the world as it is and the world as it ought to be; that our work is to narrow that chasm. To become a Bar or Bat Mitzvah is to enter the fray. It is to refuse to marginalize or ignore the suffering, to refuse to distance yourself from the pain. It is to begin to grasp the notion that every single person should be able to live a dignified life, free from oppression, poverty, and degradation. It is to recognize that your work in the world is to make this claim a reality. To become a Bar or Bat Mitzvah is to recognize that you have the capacity to bring justice and understanding to the world, to tip the scales toward comfort and consolation, peace and understanding.

Of course you don't really become an adult the day you stand before the Torah and become bat or bar mitzvah. But the journey begins that day. This book is designed to help guide you through the transition—to help you see the burning house and to give you some tools to help extinguish the fire. Use this moment as an opportunity to begin the rest of your life, so that your special day is not about the centerpieces and gifts, but about Torah and justice, your passion and commitment to the community and the world.

Mazel tov—may this experience bring abundant blessings.

Flexing Your Mitzvah Muscle

Getting Started

Is there a Bar/Bat Mitzvah in your future? Mazel tov! So much to do, so much to think about, so much to get ready for.

Traditionally, a Bar/Bat Mitzvah has three key parts. First, the Bar/Bat Mitzvah student chants a portion of the Torah at a Shabbat service. Second, he or she delivers a personal talk discussing the relevance of the Torah portion. And third, family and friends gather to celebrate after the service. Today, many families and many synagogues have added a fourth important element to the Bar/Bat Mitzvah—a mitzvah project, a service project to help others.

Are you looking for a fun and worthwhile mitzvah project? Well, this book can help you! Inside these pages, you'll find dozens and dozens of ways to connect your own interests and passions to meaningful mitzvah projects. What rocks your world? Maybe you love animals and could find homes for pets living in shelters. Maybe you're a baseball fan and could make sure kids in need have bats and gloves to play your favorite sport. Or maybe you're the best latke maker in your family and you could share your culinary skills with the hungry. It's up to you.

So Many Reasons to Help Others

Using your interests and talents to help others is actually fun. But that's not the main reason to do a mitzvah project. Here are just a few of the many, many other reasons:

- Making the world a better place is a core Jewish value.
- Helping others makes you appreciate all that you do have.
- Taking action makes you believe in yourself, that you have the spirit to make things better.
- You feel hopeful that your time, effort, and energy will make a change for the better.
- It is a great way to meet some new friends.
- Your grandmother might even call you a mensch; in Yiddish, that's a good person.

Let's remember, we are all part of one world, so by working together we can make it the best world it can be.

Every Act of Kindness Counts

As you think about shaping your mitzvah project, follow your heart. Any mitzvah project you do with love is a good deed. In Hebrew, acts of loving-kindness are called *gemilut hasadim*. Even eight hundred years ago, during the Middle Ages, Rabbi Moshe ben Maimon, known as Maimonides, one of the greatest Torah scholars, taught about the importance of giving of your time and your heart. Maimonides was a rabbi, physician, and a philosopher—and you thought you were busy! Maimonides is also famous for his writing about *tzedakah*, a Hebrew word commonly translated as "charity," but more literally meaning "justice."

How This Book Can Help You

This book will help you plan a mitzvah project that fits your talents and interests to inspire your own good deeds, or *ma'asim tovim*. In each chapter, you'll find six mitzvah projects that relate to each chapter's topic. Some chapters include many profiles of B'nai/B'not Mitzvah and their projects, some just a couple. Either way, you will find lots of ideas for making your mark on the world. Each chapter also includes journal pages for you to keep track of anything you want to remember. Be sure to flip through all the chapters. From "Operation Salami Drop" to "Cycling 4 Haiti" to "Hospital Holiday Toy Drive," you never know what might inspire you.

Finally, read through "Everyday Mitzvot: Eighteen Small Ideas That Are Big" to see how your daily acts of kindness can also help you repair the world (known as practicing *tikkun olam*). Judaism teaches us that good deeds are a lifelong commitment, not a one-time wonder.

Whatever mitzvah project you choose, sharing your talents and enthusiasm with others will make the world a better place. Imagine the impact you can make in your community and the world, for your Bar/Bat Mitzvah … and your life. One thing is certain. The world needs you!

Send Us Your Mitzvah Project Story

One last thing: Once you have completed your mitzvah project, please let us know all about it. Go to www.mitzvahprojectbook.com and send us your story so we can include it online and in future editions of this book. Sharing your story gives you one more chance to do a good deed, by inspiring others with your example.

Mitzvah Project Planning Guide

While each mitzvah project has its own unique requirements, this guide will help you get focused and organized once you've picked your project. Make a copy of this page and fill it in to start heading in the right direction.

Your Name
Mitzvah Project Description Write a brief description of your mitzvah project.
In a nutshell, I will:
Goals/Tangible Results Explain who will benefit and how they will benefit from your project.
Here's how my project will help:
Organizations Include the name of organization(s) you will support or work with.

Participants

List the people you will need to work with. Think about friends and grown-ups. Include their names, phone numbers, and e-mail addresses.

Materials Needed

List each material and quantities needed to complete your project.

To get started I will need:

Key Milestones and Dates

Note key milestones and dates for your project.

I will begin my project on:

By   , I will have

My project will be done by:

Personal Growth

Explain how you will learn and grow by completing this project.

I'll feel great when:

Mitzvah Project Ideas

Real Kids, Real Mitzvot Stories

Journal Pages

Creativity and Compassion

Arts & Crafts

"The dignity of the artist lies in his duty of keeping awake
the sense of wonder in the world."
—MARC CHAGALL (1887–1985), PAINTER

Lead Art Projects with Little Ones

Think back to the art projects you loved when you were younger. Was play dough your passion? How about stringing pasta tubes and painting them to make necklaces? Maybe it was sponge prints that unleashed your inner Chagall. Share your creativity with children at homeless shelters, day care centers, or after-school programs in your area. Contact the director to see if and when you can come in to lead art projects. If you are not permitted, offer to provide all the materials and instructions.

✓ Get It Going

Need a recipe to make your own play dough?

1 cup flour
1 cup warm water
2 teaspoons cream of tartar
1 teaspoon oil

1/4 cup salt
Food coloring

Mix all ingredients, adding food coloring last. Carefully stir over medium heat until smooth. Remove from pan and knead until blended smooth. Place in plastic bag or airtight container when cooled. The play dough will last for a long time.

Make Your Own Greeting Card Creations

Jewish New Year, Chinese New Year, Hanukkah, Kwanza, and Christmas—the holidays can be lots of fun, but also trying times for people who are ill, away from family, or under stress. So take out your markers, stickers, glitter, and paper and create your own collection of handmade cards. Be sure to write inspirational and upbeat thoughts on the inside to accompany your artwork.

✓ Get It Going

Think about people who may need a pick-me-up during the holiday season. What about children in the hospital, soup kitchen guests, or nursing home residents? Contact an appropriate administrator and explain your idea. Find out how many cards are needed to ensure that everyone receives one.

Auction Your Artwork

Does your middle school host an auction to raise money for teacher enrichment, special programs, or equipment? What better way to show your appreciation for your education than to support your school? If you are a potter, donate ceramic pieces. If you draw, you could create bookplates. Woodworkers, think about making a coat rack or step stool. These are just a few of the many items you could create to auction.

✓ Get It Going

To encourage a bidding war, be sure your item can be used or enjoyed by many people. For example, if you sew, make items such as aprons that don't need to fit perfectly to be worn. And pick fabric that both men and women would wear. Think about putting your school name on your creation, too.

Capture the Moment

Do you enjoy looking through a camera lens to create your art? Then, why not snap and sell photos to raise money for your favorite charity that supports the arts? Parents love photos of their children, especially when the photos give them glimpses of their kids that they would not typically get to see. Ask permission from your temple's education director to photograph students while at Hebrew or Sunday school. Then, organize the photos by grade level, and send an e-mail to the parents with a link to the digital photos. Ask them to make a donation for each photo they print, and be sure to tell them where you will donate the money and where to send their checks.

✓ Get It Going

Want to find art-related charities to support? There are many types, including nonprofits that provide art programs for children and adults with developmental disabilities or for homeless children. A good way to find local programs is to ask the art teacher at your school. You can also look online for national or international programs.

Create a Tree of Life

The tree of life, or *etz chaim,* is a beautiful symbol used in many religions and cultures, often relating to the unity of all life on Earth. Create your own interpretations of this universal image, and then give your creations to churches and mosques in your town to promote interfaith harmony. Include a note explaining your mitzvah project, your hopes for the world, and your artwork.

✓ Get It Going

There are so many ways to create a tree of life image—you can make a quilt, a painting, a woodblock print, a silk-screen image, a relief mural, or a wire sculpture. Just make sure to sign your name!

Craft *Tzedakah* Boxes

Tzedakah boxes, also called *pushkes*, are special containers for collecting money to give to others in need. Even more important than creating beautiful *tzedakah* boxes is putting them to good use. Give your boxes to organizations in your temple that meet regularly but that may not think about collecting money for causes. Does your temple have an adult softball team, choir, Israeli film club … ? Your box could inspire them to start each meeting with a collection for an organization that has relevance to the group.

✓ Get It Going

Here is one tried-and-true design idea. Start with a thirty-two-ounce yogurt container or can with a plastic cover. Decorate the sides with fabric, wallpaper, or beautiful paper. Add symbolic decorations using stickers, jewels, shells, ribbon, or whatever inspires you. Using a sharp knife, and working carefully under adult supervision, make a slit in the top of the plastic cover big enough to fit paper money and coins.

Real Kids, Real Mitzvot

Kate H.—Supporting Orphans through Her Craft

Family ties: Kate and her mom love to bead. Kate came up with the idea to make and sell beaded earrings to raise money for Superkids (www.adoptionsbygladney.com/html/services/human_superkids.php), an organization that sends all types of pediatric therapists (physical, occupational, speech, play) to assist children in orphanages. Kate's little sister Phoebe was adopted from China, so Kate wanted the money she raised to go to the Superkids Chinese program.

Family effort: Kate made more than one hundred pairs of earrings and sold them to neighbors, friends, and relatives. She sold earrings at her sister's birthday party as well as at a crafts fair at her temple. Through her efforts, Kate raised over $1,200, which covered the cost of a plane flight for at least one more therapist to go to China to help orphans there. Another benefit of Kate's mitzvah project is that it spread awareness of problems in Chinese orphanages.

Alex M.—Knit-a-Mitzvah

Big hands: Alex learned how to knit in an elective class taught by his math teacher. Despite his big, bulky boy hands and his tendency toward hideous handwriting, Alex took to the intricacies of knitting and quickly excelled in the class. Alex's cantor, an avid knitter herself, noticed his skill with knitting needles and suggested he choose Knit-a-Mitzvah— a weekly knitting group at his temple that makes items for area shelter residents—for his project.

Bigger heart: Alex helped knit three hundred hats in time for the Christmas dinner for shelter guests at his synagogue. He also included a note in his Bar Mitzvah invitations asking his guests to bring either knitted hats or yarn to his Bar Mitzvah. The response was overwhelming! In addition to dozens of knitted caps made by friends and family, he collected over seventy skeins of yarn, which Alex counted, sorted by color, and stuffed into the cantor's Knit-a-Mitzvah closet for future use. Guess what decorated the tables at Alex's Bar Mitzvah lunch? Knitted hats on Styrofoam heads!

Daniel W.—Forgoing Gifts to Give the Gift of Art
to Homeless Youth

It is better to give than to receive: Daniel found a way to turn his passion for art into a passion for helping homeless youth. He selected p:ear (www.pearmentor.org), an organization on the West Coast that builds positive relationships with Portland's homeless youth through education, art, and recreation to affirm personal worth and create more meaningful and healthier lives. Daniel is the youngest of four children and followed in the tradition of his brother and sisters by asking for donations to a specific charity in lieu of Bar/Bat Mitzvah gifts. Daniel's parents believe that helping others should be the focus of this coming-of-age milestone and that forgoing gifts is a first step toward living a life of mitzvot.

Where there is life there is hope: In his invitation, Daniel asked guests to make cash donations to p:ear. Daniel and his mom also bought art supplies to use for table centerpieces at his Bar Mitzvah lunch and then donated the supplies to p:ear to use in their programming. Daniel's mom acknowledges that Daniel had an occasional squeak of "Why does everyone else get presents?" But overall, Daniel was proud of the money and supplies he collected to help homeless youth.

Julia L.—Sewing Warm and Cuddly Quilts

A stitch in time: Julia's been sewing since she was eight years old. So, for her mitzvah project, she put her needlework to work for others. Julia's mom's friend is the director of REACH Beyond Domestic Violence (www.reachma.org), an organization that supports families who have experienced domestic violence. Since the organization was opening a new shelter and needed bedding, Julia sewed children's quilts to donate to REACH.

Brings comfort: Julia selected bright colors and happy prints for the quilting squares. She stitched the kid-friendly material together to make a half-dozen five-by-five-foot quilts. Together with her mom, Julia delivered the quilts to the director of REACH. That's when Julia learned that the director's plan was to give a child a quilt to take home as he or she transitioned out of the shelter to safe housing. While Julia finds sewing comforting, she hopes her quilts also bring comfort to each child receiving one of her original creations.

Cassidy G.—Weaving for Smiles

Cheering kids with cancer: As a budding artist, Cassidy picked a mitzvah project that called upon her creative talents. For a year before her Bat Mitzvah, Cassidy worked hard weaving colorful wall hangings for the walls of the Valerie Fund Children's Center for Cancer and Blood Disorders (www.saintbarnabas.com/services/valerie_fund). Cassidy wanted to help kids in her local area, and this center presented the perfect place to hang her happy artwork.

Creating what kids like: Cassidy's mom cut the chicken-wire frames that formed the base of each woven wall hanging. Cassidy spent her own money to buy the ribbons and decorations for each creation. She purchased pom-poms, rhinestones, feathers, and just about anything and everything that would make her weavings festive. Each unique wall hanging took several hours to complete. One is all sparkly with pastel colors; another uses ribbon decorated with dog bones; another reflects patriotism with red, white, and blue materials; and yet another centers around a patch of bright fire-engine red. When Cassidy completed all her weavings, she brought them to the children's center but, due to privacy concerns, wasn't able meet any of the children. Nonetheless, Cassidy felt proud of her gift. "It was a great feeling to be doing something that I knew would make kids with cancer smile," noted Cassidy.

Emily L.—A Party of Service

Let's what? Emily and her family held a Bat Mitzvah celebration that was also her mitzvah project. Following the synagogue service and brief *Kiddush* luncheon, her family and friends changed into jeans. Emily's parents arranged for transportation to take everyone to an underfunded elementary school in a neighboring town. Instead of partying, Emily's group went to work beautifying the school building and grounds!

Happy to help: For a couple of hours, about seventy-five children and fifty adults painted silhouettes of athletes and colorful words down school hallways. Some people painted line games, like hopscotch and foursquare, on the playground blacktop. Others planted gardens, and some stayed seated inside, decorating picture frames with encouraging messages ("You are a star!") for the children's school photos. Afterwards, Emily's family held a pizza party in the school's gym for her hungry helpers. Jersey Cares (www.jerseycares.org), a nonprofit organization that links volunteers to meaningful service projects, brought all the supplies and arranged the event. Emily shared, "I loved how we all came together. Everyone remembers my party because we all had fun for a cause. I hope others will take risks and try new ways to celebrate."

Arts & Crafts Journal

Let your love of art make the world a more beautiful place—
literally and figuratively.

What inspired you in this chapter? Jot down ideas you want to
remember for possible mitzvah projects … and beyond.

_____

_____

_____

_____

_____

_____

_____

_____

_____

_____

_____

_____

_____

_____

_____

_____

_____

_____

_____

_____

_____

_____

Clothes & Fashion

"One is greeted according to one's garb, bidden
farewell according to one's wisdom."

—YIDDISH FOLK SAYING

Make Shawls to Share

Some congregations ask people to wear prayer shawls, or *tallitot*,
when they come up to the bimah. Some people choose to wear
tallitot throughout the entire service. In the Reform and
Conservative movements, both men and women often wear *tallitot*.
No matter who wears a prayer shawl or when they wear it, it's always
nice to be wrapped in a beautiful one. Make your own prayer shawl
creations to give to others. Donate them to a local Jewish social
service agency to distribute to people in need. Offer them as gifts
to new members or elders in your synagogue.

✓ Get It Going

Sew, embroider, tie-dye … whatever is your specialty. You can
make a *tallit* from any material except a mixture of wool and
linen, because that weave is prohibited by the Torah.
Traditional *tallitot* are made of wool. Just don't forget to attach
the special knotted fringes, known as *tzitzit*, to the four corners.

Did you know that a *tallit* can also be used as a *chuppah*, or wedding canopy?

Donate Dresses and Suits

Are you lucky enough to wear a new dress or suit at your Bat/Bar Mitzvah? Some families are not able to afford that luxury. Collect new and gently worn dress clothing for boys and girls to wear on their special day, so they look as good as they feel when they become Bar/Bat Mitzvah. Contact your local Jewish social service agency to find out how to get the suits and dresses into the hands of kids in need.

✓ Get It Going

How can you collect the largest number of dress clothes in the shortest amount of time? Ask the religious educator at your and other local temples for a list of the boys and girls who had their Bar/Bat Mitzvah in the last two school years. Ask these kids to donate the clothes they wore to their own and other friends' B'nai/B'not Mitzvah. Chances are they have already outgrown the outfits. Also, approach the clothing stores where kids in your community go to purchase suits and dresses and ask the merchants to donate an outfit or two.

Knit One, Purl Two

Hospitals provide newborns with caps to keep the babies warm and help prevent them from dropping below their birth weight. Many hospitals depend on volunteers to knit or crochet baby hats for each and every baby born at their hospital, especially premature ones. Booties and blankets are also needed to send home with newborns and their parents. According to the U.S. Census, a baby is born in the country every seven seconds. So take out your needles and yarn, and knit and crochet away! Make sure to buy soft, machine-washable yarn for your handmade creations. The following online directories offer links to a wide range of free patterns: www.knittingpatterncentral.com

and www.crochetpatterncentral.com. Yarn and craft stores may even donate materials if you ask.

✓ Get It Going

If you'd prefer to knit hats for adults, consider knitting them for Israeli soldiers. An organization called A Package from Home offers instructions on their website for knitting and crocheting hats, and where to send them, to make sure Israeli soldiers keep warm in winter. Visit www.apackagefromhome.org.

Braid or Bead Bracelets

Do you love to make friendship bracelets? Share your jewelry creation talent with other kids so they can load up their wrists with your handmade creations. Whether you bead or braid, make bracelets in all different sizes and colors to fit the wrists and style of different-age boys and girls. Donate your unique handmade creations to children's hospitals, after-school programs, or other places where you can reach many kids.

✓ Get It Going

Take it one step further. Why not add bracelet-making materials and instructions with your gift bracelets so kids can also make their own? That way, kids can "pay it forward"—that is, repay a good deed by doing a good deed for someone else.

Stock a Thrift Shop

Create your very own collection of clothing to donate to a local thrift shop. Go beyond your own closets; ask neighbors, relatives, classmates, and even local stores to donate new and gently used items to your clothing drive. Carefully inspect all the clothing people donate. Wash and iron anything that isn't clean or pressed, sew on missing buttons, fix falling hems, and so on, and then neatly fold and hang the items before delivering them to a charitable thrift shop in your area.

✓ *Get It Going*

Check to see if there is a Hadassah thrift store anywhere near where you live. Hadassah (www.hadassah.org) is the Women's Zionist Organization of America. Hadassah supports health care, education and youth institutions, and land development in Israel. By donating to Hadassah, your donations do double duty—they provide low-cost clothing to people in need, and they raise money for Hadassah's programs.

Collect Costumes for Kids

Remember the fun you had when you were younger playing dress-up? Disco queen, princess, karate kid, superhero, fairy—all it takes is a little imagination and lots of colorful clothes for hours of enjoyment. Your job is to collect clothing and accessories to donate to a local shelter or after-school program so the kids there can have hours of fun dressing up, too. Check out if you are allowed to play with the kids. If you are, bring a camera and take photos of each of the boys and girls in their outfits, and then give each kid a print.

✓ *Get It Going*

Create a checklist of dress-up items to help friends and neighbors see that many of the clothes they have stashed in the back of their closets are actually wonderful dress-up materials. Here are a few ideas to include on your wish list: old bridesmaid's dresses, dance recital costumes, baseball pants, bathrobes, hats, shirts, ski goggles, scarves, boas, costume jewelry—anything sparkly and feathery. In fact, the more outrageous and colorful, the better.

Real Kids, Real Mitzvot

Olivia S.—Soles for Souls

Shoes make an outfit: Olivia loves shoes, but she also understands that some people don't have even one pair to adequately protect their feet. That's why Olivia chose to support Soles4Souls for her mitzvah project. Soles4Souls (www.soles4souls.org) is a charity that collects shoes to distribute free of charge to people in need in over 125 countries, including Haiti, Kenya, Thailand, Nepal, and the United States.

The more shoes the better: Olivia and her mom approached an independent shoe store in their town to ask if it would be a drop-off center for donated shoes. Not only did the store agree, but it also donated one hundred pairs of shoes and shipped the shoes to Soles4Souls' distribution center. To spread the word, Olivia wrote an article for her local newspaper about her mitzvah project and included a note in her Bat Mitzvah invitation asking guests to bring a pair of new or gently used shoes to her Bat Mitzvah for Soles4Souls. Can you guess what Olivia's table decorations were? Shoes she and her mom bought to donate, of course!

Sarah R.—Knitting for Warmth and Smiles

Crafts that care: Sarah, her sister, and her mom spend lots of their spare time knitting. Sometimes they knit scarves, sometimes they make doll clothes, other times they work on sweaters. When Sarah thought about her mitzvah project, she wanted to put her skill with knitting needles to use. Through the Internet, she and her mom learned about a

Jewish organization in New York that collects knitted caps, called "chemo caps," for kids with cancer who have lost their hair as a result of chemotherapy and/or radiation treatments. Project found!

It's a knitzvah: Sarah chose bright, funky colors to use for the caps. She used special needles that are attached by a piece of plastic, called circular needles, to properly make the circular caps. Each month, for the ten months prior to her Bat Mitzvah, Sarah completed a chemo cap. Each one was a completely different design, but vibrant and colorful. Sarah hoped the kids liked their caps as much as she liked making them: "I hope the kids thought their caps were cool."

Morgan M.—Headbands for Cancer Research

Passion for fashion: Morgan's mother is co-owner of a women's activewear clothing store, so Morgan has grown up appreciating trendy outfits and beautiful clothes. But when it came time to think about her mitzvah project, Morgan knew that she wanted the project to honor her grandmother, who had passed away from cancer of the bone marrow. It was Morgan's Hebrew school tutor who actually nudged her in the direction of her project that combined both priorities. One day, her tutor commented, "Morgan, every day you wear such cute headbands. They are really your trademark." That got Morgan thinking. She decided she could sell headbands to raise money for bone marrow cancer research.

Selling for charity: At first, Morgan and her mom thought about making headbands. But then they realized Morgan could buy and resell manufactured headbands. They ordered stretchy, pink tie-dyed ones from a company in Florida called Pretty Please. All the money Morgan raised went to the charity, because her family paid their wholesale cost. Morgan promoted her project by explaining it to her friends online. Many of her camp friends in other states placed orders. Her school friends also bought the headbands. In addition, Morgan sold the bands at her mom's store and advertised the effort with a handmade poster in the shop's window. "I love seeing my friends wearing their tie-dyed headbands, because it makes me feel good to know I'm helping such an important cause," she explained.

Eva L.—Raising Funds with Handmade Bracelets

On the run: Eva is always busy—three seasons of sports, Jewish youth group, studying, socializing… So she picked a mitzvah project she could accomplish in between activities at all times of night and day. Eva designed, strung, and sold large faux-pearl bracelets on a choice of pink, black, or white ribbon to raise money for a homeless shelter.

In style: Eva sent out e-mails with a photo of her fashionable bracelets and an order form to all the girls and women she and her mom could think of. Her design was a hit. Eva raised over a $1,000, which she donated in person to the shelter.

Kayla B.—Collecting Pajamas for Cozy Bedtimes

Why PJs? Through her school's involvement with a homeless shelter, Kayla learned about many issues homeless families face. Her class served meals to homeless people once a month, and the students were encouraged to make eye contact and connect with those they were helping. In addition, a former homeless woman came to speak to Kayla's class about her experience. But it was in a class discussion about *tzedakah,* when the writer Danny Siegel talked about a homeless child who received his very first pair of pajamas from a donation, that Kayla came up with the idea for her mitzvah project. Kayla was surprised and saddened to hear that a child didn't even know what PJs were, because he had never seen them before. Kayla decided to collect PJs for children at a shelter in her area.

Sweeter dreams: Kayla's mom helped her contact a local organization, a "safe house" for kids escaping from domestic abuse, to see if there was a need for pajamas. The group, New Beginnings (www.newbegin.org), was very excited by the idea. Kayla enlisted the help of her Girl Scout troop, her school, and her synagogue to collect donations of PJs. She also hosted a sleepover party and asked her friends to bring gently used PJs to donate. She sorted through all the PJs to make sure they were clean and in good shape and then folded them neatly. Kayla donated over one hundred pairs of pajamas. Kayla enjoyed delivering the many bags of PJs to the New Beginnings office, hopeful that "the kids feel a bit more secure and happier wearing cozy PJs to bed."

Clothes & Fashion Journal

Helping others is always in style. So, if clothing and accessories are your passions, share your personal style with others.

What inspired you in this chapter? Jot down ideas you want to remember for possible mitzvah projects ... and beyond.

Computers & Technology

"Obviously everyone wants to be successful, but I want to be looked back on as being very innovative, very trusted, and ethical and ultimately making a big difference in the world."
—SERGEY BRIN, GOOGLE CO-FOUNDER

Help Drivers Save Money and the Environment

Did you know that a simple tire gauge can help protect the environment? Who said all technology has to be complicated! If tires are inflated to the proper level, vehicles run more efficiently and use less gas. If you care about reducing oil drilling, global warming, and dependence on foreign countries, then spread the word about proper tire inflation. You could host free tire-reading clinics in parking lots at your school when parents are there for sporting events. You could pass out flyers and send out e-mails to friends and neighbors to raise awareness for the clinic or simply about the benefits of proper tire pressure in general. You could even hold a raffle for tire gauges and donate the money you raise to an environmental cause.

✓ Get It Going

Need some facts about proper tire inflation? Start here: Always use the vehicle manufacturer's guidelines for proper tire inflation.

Look for the information in your car owner's manual, on the inside of the glove-box door, or posted on the edge of the driver's-side door. Radial tires are supposed to have a slight bulge in the sidewall at their proper inflation pressure. Check your tire pressure every month and especially before a long trip or pulling a heavy load. To make sure you get an accurate reading, check tires when they're cold, that is, when your vehicle has not been used for at least three hours. Last but not least, use a reliable gauge.

Turn e-Trash into *Tzedakah*

To raise money for your favorite charity, help your friends and neighbors get rid of stuff they don't need. Old electronics, such as cell phones, DVD players, TVs, and computers, often just collect dust in basements and attics. Contact an organization like EcoPhones (www.ecophones.com) to earn cash for cell phones, PDAs (personal digital assistants), and ink-jet cartridges as well as to keep hazardous materials out of landfills.

✔ Get It Going

Want to support the environment and Israel at the same time? Consider donating proceeds from your recycling efforts to environmental agencies in Israel. You can find a list at www.coejl.org/resources/israelorg.php.

Hold Cell Phone Tutorials

It's likely you're a whiz at using your cell phone for everything from talking, to texting, to taking photos. But for people who didn't grow up using cell phones, figuring out all the functions can be intimidating. You can help people learn how to charge their phone, set ringtones, enter and save phone numbers, text, take and send photos—all the things you do daily. Offer your services for free to adults in your temple or at your town's senior center. A half-hour one-on-one lesson will go a long way in making people more adept at using their phone.

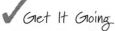 Get It Going

Be sure to inform every adult you tutor about your state's cell phone and text messaging laws. Since more and more states are prohibiting drivers from using handheld cell phones and from text messaging while driving, check the Governors Highway Safety Association for up-to-date information at www.ghsa.org and click on link for cell phone laws on the home page.

Donate Your Computer Services

Are you good at desktop publishing—creating graphics, using special text effects, and incorporating photos into documents? Can you design HTML e-mails or websites? What about creating spreadsheets or databases? Whatever your computer expertise, offer your services to nonprofit organizations or people doing good deeds that may need your help.

✔ Get It Going

Is there a community service group in your school? Is your younger sister or brother in a Girl or Boy Scout troop? Is your mom or dad or one of your friends' moms or dads supporting a cause you believe in? These are just a few of the people and groups that could use your computer savvy to help others.

Digitize Piles of Print Photos

Many adults have boxes and boxes of print photographs that they took over many years before digital photography gained popularity. Help people preserve precious memories by scanning their photos and creating digitized photo files on their computer. You could offer this service to relatives and to adults in your neighborhood or at your synagogue.

✔ Get It Going

Take it a step further. Why not suggest buying a digital photo frame so the favorite photos you've just digitized are always within eyesight? Then load the favorite photos in the frame, and even offer to come back a couple of times a year to update the selection.

Help Bring Green Israeli Technology to Remote African Villages

Now you can support Israeli technology and African villagers at the same time. Since 2008, Jewish Heart for Africa (www.jhasol.org) has applied Israeli innovation to improving African lives. How? By bringing solar-powered light, clean water, and refrigeration for life-saving vaccines to villagers in Ethiopia, Tanzania, and Uganda. So, if you're enthusiastic about green technology, why not raise money for Jewish Heart for Africa? Collect returnable bottles and cans from your relatives, neighbors, and classmates to raise funds to donate. Spread the word about why you are collecting bottles and cans, and where and when you'll be collecting.

✓ Get It Going

When selecting a charity to support, consider how much of the money you donate actually goes to helping others versus to business costs of running the charity. You want to be sure that the organization you put your dollars behind is run efficiently. One hundred percent of the money you donate to Jewish Heart for Africa goes directly to the organization's projects in Africa, since foundations support its operating costs.

Real Kids, Real Mitzvot

Jason G.—Turning Techie Skills into Tzedakah

Personal computer: Jason's the go-to guy whenever one of his friends or family members has a question or problem using a computer. He knows how to load software, diagnose network issues, and create spreadsheets, databases, and graphics, plus so much more.

Personal commitment: For his mitzvah project, Jason wanted to make a difference in Darfur, a country where more than two million people have been forced from their homes. Jason heard about the Darfur Stoves Project (www.darfurstoves.org), an organization that provides Darfuri women with fuel-efficient stoves. Because the stoves require less firewood, women decrease their exposure to violence while collecting wood as well as their need to trade food rations for fuel. To raise money for the organization, Jason sold his computer services. Jason got the word out by e-mail, of course, as well as through word of mouth. He donated the money he earned and some of the money he received for his Bar Mitzvah to purchase multiple $20 stoves. Not only does a $20 stove reduce exposure to violence, it also saves a woman a dollar a day, and reduces emissions of greenhouse gases by eight tons over five years. Now, that's truly a case of a little bit of money going a long way.

Max S.—High Holy Days Broadcast

Share the service: Max used his technology skills to broadcast his synagogue's High Holy Day services for his Bar Mitzvah project. Initially, the broadcast was intended to serve a single temple member with cancer who had a stem-cell transplant and could not be in crowds. When Max's synagogue publicized the upcoming broadcast, it had unexpected benefits. Many older temple members, and even non-temple members, found and enjoyed the broadcast online.

High-Tech High Holy Days: Max used equipment including a Windows computer with a Logitech webcam, a Verizon wireless modem adapter, and a Ustream.tv to stream the video from the webcam over the Internet. On Erev Rosh

Hashanah, Max's rabbi introduced him and explained what he would be doing, so no congregants would be concerned seeing Max filming with a small camera in the sanctuary. Quite the contrary—the synagogue received many letters praising Max's contemporary concept. One person wrote, "I just had my second hip surgery on September 1. I hope you can do more innovative things like Max's Bar Mitzvah project. It really worked. I even followed along in my prayer book. Again, a heartfelt thanks."

Computers & Technology Journal

U can make G8 things happen when u use technology
for the G8r good.

What inspired you in this chapter? Jot down ideas you want to
remember for possible mitzvah projects ... and beyond.

_____

_____

_____

_____

_____

_____

_____

_____

_____

_____

_____

_____

_____

_____

_____

_____

_____

_____

_____

_____

Food & Cooking

"When you reap the harvest of your land, do not reap to the very edges of your field or gather the gleanings of your harvest. Leave them for the poor and the alien."

—LEVITICUS 23:22

Doctor Up Some Jewish Penicillin

Many say that chicken soup heals the body and the soul. Cooking multiple batches of soup to deliver to synagogue members who are sick is truly a mitzvah. Freeze the soup in portions ready to be delivered to young and old who are in need of healing. Check if your temple has a Caring Committee that coordinates food delivery to temple members who are ill. You could even include a get-well note with each serving.

✓ Get It Going

Not yet a person who cooks from experience without recipes or measuring? Then consult a Jewish cookbook for a fail-proof soup recipe. *Cooking Jewish: 532 Great Recipes from the Rabinowitz Family, Healthy Jewish Cooking, Joan Nathan's Jewish Holiday Cookbook, The Book of Jewish Food*, and *The New York Times Jewish Cookbook* are just a few of your options. Visit your local bookstore, www.amazon.com, www.bn.com, or your synagogue's library and gift shop for more cookbook ideas.

Make a Case for Baskets

Are you a "foodie"? Why not assemble baskets of specialty foods for table centerpieces at your Bar/Bat Mitzvah celebration and donate them after the lunch or dinner? They are a great way to express your passion and provide treats to families in need at the same time. Food pantries, shelters for the homeless or battered women, and group homes for disabled citizens are just a few of the organizations that would likely love to receive your gift.

✔ Get It Going

Dried fruit, crackers, soup, candy, tea/coffee, and jam are some of the nonperishable items you can package up. Citrus fruit, canned fish, nuts, cheese, and cookies also work well. Make sure each basket has food that is delicious and nutritious. Pick items that are colorful with varied shapes to arrange at different heights. Wrap it all up with cellophane, tie a beautiful bow, and include a note with the name of the organization to receive the basket.

Bake Challahs for New Immigrants

At one point in time, our families were all new immigrants in America. Today, many new Jewish immigrants are from Russia and the Newly Independent States (formerly part of the USSR, the Union of Soviet Socialist Republics), such as Ukraine, Byelorussia, Latvia, and Kazakhstan. Making a "Shabbat Welcome Kit" is a lovely way to help ease the transition to a new home. Bake challahs and package them with a challah cover, Shabbat candlesticks, and candles. Or make an entire Shabbat dinner, adding roasted chicken, soup, vegetables, and dessert as well.

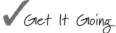 **Get It Going**

Many Jewish Family & Children's Service agencies provide services to support new immigrants. The Hebrew Immigrant Aid Society, HIAS (www.hias.org), is the international migration agency of the American Jewish community, providing rescue for persecuted and oppressed Jews around the world, including Sergey Brin, who would go on to become co-founder of Google. Check with a social service agency in your area to find families to welcome with Shabbat challahs and more.

Stock a Kitchen

As women, men, and families move from homeless shelters or group housing to homes of their own, they often need table- and cookware. Contact the Department of Health and Human Services in your state or a local shelter to inquire about the needs of their clients moving into independent living. Once you have a list, there are lots of ways for you to collect these items. Canvas your neighbors, friends, synagogue members, and family with flyers and e-mails asking for donations of gently used items on your list. Approach housewares stores to solicit donations of sale or discontinued items. Ask restaurants, caterers, and rental agencies for donations of table- and cookware as well.

✔ **Get It Going**

What basics does a well-stocked kitchen need? Typically, a set of dishes, glasses, mugs, and silverware for six; a skillet; a one- or two-quart saucepan; a large pot for boiling pasta; a rectangular and a round casserole dish for roasting/baking; three mixing bowls; a serving fork and spoon; an oven mitt; kitchen towels; a spatula; a set of measuring cups and spoons; a mixing spoon; and a paring, a bread, and a chef's knife. A checklist will certainly help you keep track of what you've collected and what you need!

Compile a Cookbook

When you gather traditional recipes from Jewish seniors, you capture culture and heritage for generations to come. Reach out to elders in your synagogue, neighborhood, and family for their favorite dishes. When you collect the recipes, make sure to ask about special memories associated with each one so you can annotate entries with living history. Type up the recipes, include photos and graphics, and of course, credit the chefs who contributed. You could give copies to all the kids in your Hebrew school class and, certainly, to all those who contributed to your cookbook, too! Or maybe sell the cookbooks and earn money to donate to Meals on Wheels for seniors. Locate a local Meals on Wheels at "Find a Meal" at www.mowaa.org.

✔ Get It Going

There are many creative ways to organize your cookbook. There's the standard approach, by course—appetizers, main dishes, side dishes, desserts. How about by country of origin, such as recipes from Russia, Poland, America, and Israel? Consider organizing by Jewish holiday, including Shabbat, Hanukkah, Passover, and Rosh Hashanah, or organize the recipes into special memories, such as family dinners, party food, car food, summer fun, lunchbox favorites, and comfort food for healing.

Be a Brunch Buddy

Eating alone day after day can be lonely for people who enjoy company. Do you have a neighbor or member of your synagogue who lives alone? Why not offer to join him or her for Sunday brunch once a month? Fruit salad, bagels, lox, cream cheese, coffee cake, and muffins are just a few of the dishes you could prepare. Whether you eat at your house or at your brunch buddy's, it's important that your parents or trusted adults in your synagogue know this person before you offer your company to ensure that it's a safe, good fit.

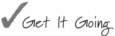 Get It Going

Are you concerned about conversation topics? It's likely that conversation will flow naturally once you get to know this person just a little. Be sure to ask questions to learn about your brunch buddy's past and current life, being conscious of what he or she is comfortable speaking about.

Real Kids, Real Mitzvot

Emma S.—Sweet Tooth Fairy

Saving the best for last: Ice cream, chocolate chip cookies, brownies, and fudge all top Emma's list of sweet treats—of course, after she eats her healthy food. Emma decided to share her love of dessert with other kids for her mitzvah project.

Putting sugar to good use: Emma and a friend ran a make-your-own ice-cream sundae party for kids at a homeless shelter. She also helped decorate hundreds of gingerbread cookies for children attending a holiday party hosted by an organization that provides services to families who have experienced domestic violence. In addition, Emma and another friend got permission from the principal of their middle school to have a bake sale after school to raise money for their mitzvah projects. Emma donated her portion of the proceeds to the Cotting School (www.cotting.org), a school outside of Boston for special-needs children that she saw a segment about on TV. Sometimes, desserts can be good for health—especially when they make children smile!

Josh R.—Fighting Hunger

Sorting, stacking, and scanning: As part of becoming a Bar Mitzvah, Josh volunteered at the Greater Boston Food Bank (www.gbfb.org), which distributes both fresh and nonperishable food to hunger-relief agencies throughout Boston. He helped sort or catalog almost fifty-four thousand pounds of food to help feed hungry people in eastern Massachusetts. Josh's favorite jobs were organizing the pasta, soup cans, and other surplus foods and scanning boxes of dry foods to make sure they were the right weight.

Carrying on a tradition of service: Working at the food bank reminded Josh how fortunate he and his family are. They eat well, sleep in a warm house, and attend fantastic schools. Josh was pleased to be able to carry on the social action tradition that has been part of both sides of his family for generations.

Alison H.—Happy Holiday Cookie Bakers

Mixing it up: Can you imagine baking 250 gingerbread cookies ... and not eating a single one? (Well, maybe just one!) That's what Alison did as part of her mitzvah project to make sure families supported by an organization that provides services to women, men, and children who have experienced domestic violence would enjoy a sweet treat at a holiday party in their honor. With the help of her mom and sister, she spent a weekend mixing batter, rolling dough, cutting out gingerbread men with cookie cutters, and baking the cookies to perfection.

Many hands make light work: To get help decorating the cookies, Allison turned to friends, some also working on their Bat Mitzvah projects. Out came the frosting glaze, shredded coconut, chocolate chips, colorful sugar, and sprinkles. The finished cookies were a big hit with the children at the holiday party—not to mention the adults, too.

Michael K.—Cooking Up Community Support

Hot food: After long days at school and afternoon sports practices, Michael enjoys helping his parents prepare dinner. But for his mitzvah project, one night a month Michael helped prepare dinner at a nearby soup kitchen instead. He made salads; watched over pasta, soup, and chicken dishes as they were cooking; and served thirty to forty guests their dinners. Once the guests were finished eating, Michael scrubbed pots, pans, and cooking utensils.

Warm spirit: As Michael readily admitted, until volunteering at the soup kitchen, he took for granted that he would have a hot meal each evening. For many of the elders, mothers, and children, as well as the other guests he served, this was their only hot dinner of the entire week. After his mitzvah project, Michael is much more appreciative of dinners with family and other simple pleasures.

Leah S.—Creating a Club to Feed Others

Bon appétit: In seventh grade, Leah S. and a group of six other Jewish friends from middle school decided to form a mitzvah cooking group. On the second Sunday of each month at 2:00 p.m., the girls got together to cook a meal for about thirty homeless men. The families rotated hosting "the chefs," and the host girl planned the menu and helped with shopping. The host parents then delivered the tasty and wholesome food to a local shelter that afternoon.

Too many cooks don't spoil the broth! The cooking club is still in existence three years later, with the girls in ninth grade, and a non-Jewish friend has joined as well. Recipes come from cookbooks and the Internet—chili and lasagna are group specialties. In addition to dinners, the girls have expanded the menu to include muffins, which can be

frozen and eaten another day for breakfast. Leah S. was surprised—what started out as doing something for others also
benefits the girls themselves: "Now we're in high school
and hardly have time to see each other, so our cooking club
gives us a chance to catch up and have fun!"

Jessica K.—Serving Meals with Dignity

At the Jubilee Café: Jessica and her mom learned about
the Jubilee Café from a friend. The Jubilee Café serves
restaurant-style breakfast to in-need community members
every Tuesday and Friday morning in a local church. Since
the café is a joint venture between the University of Kansas
and the town of Lawrence, most volunteers are college students. In the summer when students leave campus, the
number of volunteers dwindles, so the café is in desperate
need of help. Jessica knew this would be a place where she
could help.

Doing it all over time: Jessica began volunteering the summer before her Bat Mitzvah, from 6:00 to 9:00 a.m., and has
continued helping each summer since then. Over time, she
has learned nearly every job at the café: she has cooked
eggs, biscuits, pancakes, hash browns, and toast; set up the
dining room; cleared the dining room; served food; and
loaded the industrial sanitizer. In her second summer at
the café, Jessica earned a blue nametag, which designates
her as a "regular." She also donated 10 percent of her Bat
Mitzvah gifts to the Jubilee Café and has recruited several
of her friends to help in the kitchen, too. Jessica explains
what her mitzvah project has taught her: "In the beginning,
I did not really understand the importance of that hot meal
twice a week. Now, I appreciate everything that I have and
all the opportunities I've been given."

Justin C.—Dining for Dollars

Fight against hunger: When Justin and his mom brainstormed topics for his mitzvah project, he settled on the idea of fighting hunger. Justin had recently learned about MAZON: A Jewish Response to Hunger (www.mazon.org), a nonprofit organization that donates $4 million yearly to food banks mainly in the United States, but also across the world. MAZON encourages people to include MAZON in their life-cycle celebrations and offers a "Bar/Bat Mitzvah *Tzedakah* Project Manual" on its website.

Pay what you want: Jason organized a spaghetti dinner at his synagogue to raise donations and to bring together people for a fun meal. He "advertised" it to his friends online, his school friends, and his synagogue community. He, his mom, and his sister boiled thirty-two pounds of pasta, warmed fifteen loaves of garlic bread, mixed six tubs of salad, and baked over two hundred cookies! The dinner was attended by 118 people, who donated more than $2,000. Justin sent all the money to MAZON to fight hunger and to feed the people in Haiti who had just suffered a devastating earthquake. Jason's favorite part of the event was after the dinner: "I had hoped to raise $500, but was amazed that the total was over four times that! It showed me how generous people can be when they come together for an important cause."

Food & Cooking Journal

You don't need to be a professional chef to cook up projects
that warm the hearts and stomachs of people in need.

What inspired you in this chapter? Jot down ideas you want to
remember for possible mitzvah projects … and beyond.

_____

_____

_____

_____

_____

_____

_____

_____

_____

_____

_____

_____

_____

_____

_____

_____

_____

_____

_____

_____

Movies & Drama

"From a very young age, my parents taught me the most important lesson of my whole life: They taught me how to listen. They taught me how to listen before I made up my own mind. When you listen, you learn."

—STEVEN SPIELBERG, DIRECTOR, SCREENWRITER, PRODUCER, AND FOUNDER OF THE USC SHOAH FOUNDATION INSTITUTE

Entertain Little Kids
While Parents Attend Shabbat Services

You can be responsible for getting Shabbat off to a great start for parents of young children. Organize babysitting services at your synagogue one Friday night a month so parents can relax and enjoy Shabbat services without little kids wiggling by their sides. Speak to adults who work at your synagogue to help you plan activities and manage logistics, such as spreading the word to congregants, handling the registration process, and snack selection. Get other kids to help you, including high-school-aged members, so there is an appropriate ratio of babysitters to kids. If your synagogue already has an established babysitting service, then volunteer to help and organize skits, sing-alongs and other fun activities.

✓ Get It Going

Hosting craft projects and skits is one way to keep kids happy while their parents are at services. Organize the craft and skit around a theme, such as a Jewish holiday, an animal, or a TV ad for a made-up product, such as a robot that cleans your room. Once you pick your theme, have all the kids make masks or props for the skits. Then have the older kids create short skits to entertain the little ones. Don't forget a snack ... maybe challah and grape juice.

Broadcast Your P-O-V on a YouTube Video

Do you have a P-O-V—a point of view—about something you'd like to communicate with as many people as possible? Perhaps it is a novel idea for how to save energy. Maybe it is a government policy issue you'd like to comment on. Or maybe it is about something more personal, such as anti-bullying. How about an inspirational idea for making the world a happier place? Whatever you are compelled to communicate about, make a video to post on YouTube to spread your ideas across the digital universe.

✓ Get It Going

Make sure you maintain your privacy online. Do not include your last name, address, phone number, e-mail address, or IM address in your video.

Promote Jewish Films

A Jewish film examines some aspect of being Jewish and features at least one central Jewish character. Have you seen *Fiddler on the Roof, The Chosen, Funny Girl,* or *The Ten Commandments*? Organize a Jewish film club to show Jewish films to kids your age. Ergo Media (www.ergomedia.com) is a good resource for finding Jewish films. They have over three hundred, including children's videos, documentaries, "how-to" videos, Israeli and Yiddish film classics, educational programs, and music/art videos. If you charge a small membership fee to join your film club, you can donate the proceeds to aspiring Jewish filmmakers. Pop some popcorn, pull out the pillows, and let the show begin.

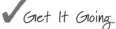 Get It Going

There are several organizations you can fund to help Jewish-themed films and filmmakers get the broadest exposure possible. The National Center for Jewish Film (www.brandeis.edu/jewishfilm) maintains the largest collection and restores old films, including Yiddish cinema. Or look to see if there is a Jewish film festival in a city close to you to which you can donate. Atlanta, Hartford, Charlottesville, Fresno, Seattle, San Francisco, Washington, D.C., and Boston are among the cities that host festivals.

Prove That Middle School Kids Can Make a Difference

Paper Clips is a project by middle school students from the small city of Whitwell, Tennessee, who were struggling to grasp the concept of six million World War II Holocaust victims. This eighth-grade project earned worldwide attention, and *Paper Clips*, the award-winning documentary film about the project, was released by Miramax Films in 2004. The uplifting movie features interviews with students, teachers, Holocaust survivors, and famous people who participated in the project. Invite your Jewish and non-Jewish friends over to watch *Paper Clips*, and show your friends how middle school kids really can make a difference.

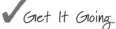 Get It Going

After you watch the movie, get your friends talking about how you all can make a difference in the world. See if you can engage the group in coming up with a specific project to help others. It could be as simple as each friend buying a new pair of socks for kids at a homeless shelter, writing a letter on behalf of a prisoner of conscience—a person who has been jailed because of his or her beliefs, ethnic origin, language, national or social origin, economic status, or other status—or donating a month of his or her allowance to a charity you agree upon as a group.

Put on a Purim Production

You can raise money for a cause you care about by organizing entertainment at Purim, a holiday when Jews traditionally put on a Purim *shpiel*, or play. Because laughter, characters, and costumes are important parts of the Purim celebration, let your imagination go a little wild! Producing a play that tells the traditional story of Purim is one way to go. Or you could write a funny skit that takes on the latke-hamantaschen debate: Which is the tastiest Jewish holiday food? What about a Purim puppet show, fashion show, or costume contest?

✓ Get It Going

Does your synagogue or local Jewish Community Center host a Purim carnival? If so, that gathering would be a logical venue for your entertainment. Ask the carnival organizer if you can be part of their festivities. Once you have the logistics arranged, recruit a few theatrical friends and their parents to help you. And to raise money for charity from your production, why not ask your audience for donations instead of selling admission tickets? Remember to spread the word about the organization for which you are raising funds. You could easily do this with posters and printed materials, and speak briefly about the charity at the end of your production. Then people will be more likely to be generous.

Organize Good Wishes to Student Actors to Do "Good" for Others

Here's a way to let people congratulate students in your school's play(s) and raise funds for charity at the same time. Speak to the head of your school's performing arts department or your principal about organizing a program where family and friends can send congratulations to any actor, musician, dancer, stage crew member, or staff member who is part of the performance. Charge a dollar to deliver a note at intermission or at the end of the play. Set up a table outside the auditorium with paper and pens. Be sure to promote your service before the performance to both students and parents, and have a big sign at your table at the performance. Remember to describe the charity the money will be donated to as well as list the cost per note. Break a leg!

✓ Get It Going

While you can choose any charity for your proceeds, you might want to pick one that relates to the theater. One approach is to donate the money to a community-based nonprofit theater company in your area that you'd like to help thrive. Or you could pick a national nonprofit such as Broadway Cares / Equity Fights AIDS (www.broadwaycares.org) or the Theatre Development Fund (www.tdf.org), which supports theatrical works of artistic merit and encourages and enables diverse audiences to attend live theater and dance.

Real Kids, Real Mitzvot

Dan S.—Filming a Legacy for the Next Generation

Befriending a survivor: Dan went with his family to an exhibit at his local Jewish Community Center called "Memories Through History." It detailed individual stories and memorabilia from Holocaust survivors who immigrated to New Jersey. One panel of information about a particular man stood out to Dan. He wanted to find out more about this man's story. He reached out and thus began a friendship. The two met on ten occasions. Each time Dan visited the survivor's home, he interviewed him. During one of the visits, he also made a video recording. Dan created the video to preserve and honor the survivor's story for generations to come.

A twin Bar Mitzvah: The survivor attended Dan's Bar Mitzvah. At the point in the ceremony when Dan received his Bar Mitzvah certificate, the rabbi also called up the gentleman. He, too, was given his own Bar Mitzvah certificate, to substitute for the one he was never able to have because of the Nazi regime. A year later, Dan and his friend organized a trip for eighth graders from Dan's public school to go to Washington, D.C. Together they visited the United States Holocaust Memorial Museum and toured the Lincoln Memorial. Dan said, "This project taught me not to be a bystander and to stand up when you see injustice."

Daniella D.—Teaching Drama and Dance

Show stopper: Daniella is a big performer. She loves dancing, drama, and music and participates in lots of acting workshops and many, many dance classes. Knowing how lucky she is to enjoy these activities, Daniella decided to offer a drama and dance class to younger kids in need as her mitzvah project.

The show goes on: Once a week over two months, Daniella volunteered to host an hour-long performance class at the Mar Vista Family Center (www.marvistafc.org), a community center where low-income kids can get a hot meal, complete homework after school, exercise, or work on computers. Daniella's mom helped her arrange for an empty room there. Equipped with a boom box and a different CD each week, Daniella hosted about a dozen kids, ages six to eleven. They played "freeze" dance, tried out simple acting games, and danced up a storm. Daniella described her biggest challenge: "Many of the kids didn't speak English, but hand movements and music are universal languages." At the final class, everyone was late and Daniella worried that the kids had forgotten to come. But they walked in one by one, each with a flower to show their appreciation for their student teacher.

Movies & Drama Journal

Plot your mitzvah project from beginning to end.
Lights, camera, action!

What inspired you in this chapter? Jot down ideas you want to remember for possible mitzvah projects ... and beyond.

_____

_____

_____

_____

_____

_____

_____

_____

_____

_____

_____

_____

_____

_____

_____

_____

_____

_____

ADMIT
ONE

Reading & Writing

"One man's candle is a light for many."
—TALMUD, BAVA BATRA

Read to Elders

Often elderly people's eyesight fails, and it is hard for them to read more than a page or so at a time, if at all. Volunteer to read newspapers, magazines, and books to help elders stay connected to the world around them. Your companionship will likely be valued as much as, if not more than, your words.

✔ *Get It Going*

Is there a retirement community, nursing home, elder day care, or town senior center near where you live? If so, call and ask to speak to a program coordinator and offer your assistance. Be sure to be clear about how often and what times you are available. When you meet the elder or elders you will be reading to, find out what they would most like to hear. Offer to go to the library to get the magazine or book they are interested in.

Write to Wounded Soldiers

It is virtually impossible to imagine the physical and emotional challenges wounded veterans face. The United Service Organizations (USO) is a nonprofit organization chartered by Congress that relies on individuals and corporations to bring comfort and recreation to the men and women in the military. You can send five hundred character e-mail messages of gratitude and wishes for health to wounded soldiers through the USO. Go to www.uso.org. Commit to a monthly or biweekly schedule of message writing. Use your way with words to bring hope and show appreciation to others.

✓ Get It Going

Take a look at these messages already sent to service members to spark ideas for how to craft your own e-mails:

- "I wake up in the morning, clueless to the challenges you must face each day. My day is filled with curious exploration with each creative expression through music. I thank YOU for that freedom." (Benjamin F., Texas)

- "I just want to say thank you guys so much for what you are doing for us each and every day! I'm sixteen years old and can't imagine what it would be like. This world needs braver people, and you guys are protecting our freedom! Thank you for everything each and every one of you do every day. God bless you all!" (Victoria S., Kansas)

Strengthen Israel's Brain Power by Using Your Own

All countries depend on the brainpower of their citizens to fuel their economies, and that's why the education of children is critical. PUSH (www.pushedu.org), an Israeli nonprofit organization staffed by volunteers, tutors over one thousand at-risk eight- to eighteen-year-old children in about one hundred Israeli public schools in sixteen towns. Many of the students are from new immigrant families from the former Soviet Union and Ethiopia. You can help support PUSH by organizing a reading pledge drive for yourself and even for your other classmates. Have the readers contact relatives, family friends, and neighbors to pledge a dollar amount for each book they read over three months. Create a digital flyer for your friends to send out explaining PUSH's mission and to solicit support.

✓ Get It Going

To learn more about PUSH and for details to use in your e-mail solicitation, go to www.pushedu.org or e-mail push11@netvision.net.il. If PUSH doesn't seem right for you, then look online or talk to people who are familiar with educational programs in Israel to find another organization you feel good about supporting.

Volunteer at the Public Library

Public libraries are great equalizers in society. They serve rich and poor, old and young, the highly educated and those without college degrees. So volunteering at a library can satisfy not only your love of books, but also your commitment to community service. The oldest library in America was started by a four-hundred-book donation by a Massachusetts clergyman, John Harvard, to a new university. (Yes, you guessed it; we're talking about Harvard University in Cambridge, Massachusetts.) But it wasn't until 1833 in Peterborough, New Hampshire, that the first public library in the country opened. Between 1881 and 1919, philanthropist Andrew Carnegie helped build more than 1,700 public libraries in the United States. According to the American Library Association, today there are more than 16,500 libraries in the United States.

✓ Get It Going

Speak to the head librarian about what kind of help is needed from volunteers. Here are some suggestions to offer: shelve books, DVDs, and CDs; read to preschoolers in the library reading room; mend books; and assist at the children's librarian reference desk.

Start an Intergenerational Book Group

Have you ever been in a book group? If you have, it is likely that the other members are kids your age and perhaps parents, too. This time, include elders—grandparents, neighbors, and great aunts and uncles—so that you have three generations of members in your group. Every participant will benefit from different perspectives, rich discussion, and new friendships.

✓ Get It Going

Need some suggestions for books to read in your intergenerational book group? Pick books at a middle-school reading level that all ages will enjoy. Make sure they are thought-provoking enough to lead to interesting discussions. Check out *Diary of a Young Girl*, by Anne Frank; *Habibi*, by Naomi Shihab Nye; *The Night Journey*, by Kathryn Lasky; *Roll of Thunder, Hear My Cry*, by Mildred D. Taylor; *The Upstairs Room*, by Johanna Reiss; *To Kill a Mockingbird*, by Harper Lee; *The Outsiders*, by S. E. Hinton; and *Island of the Blue Dolphins*, by Scott O'Dell.

Interview Holocaust Survivors

Over sixty years have passed since the liberation of the Nazi concentration camps at the end of World War II. While history books document the deaths of six million Jews in the Holocaust, soon kids will not have the chance to meet a Holocaust survivor, as they will all have died of old age. What an incredible honor and mitzvah to interview elders who survived the Holocaust either by living through a concentration camp, hiding from the Nazis, or fleeing their home country. By preserving Holocaust survivors' memories, you help to ensure that terrible atrocities done to people are not denied or repeated. Bring a recorder so you can produce both an oral and a written history to share with others.

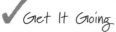 Get It Going

The most important thing to remember when you conduct your interviews is to take the lead from the survivors. You may start by asking them what they would like to speak about. If you see that their memory is failing, move on to an area that they are comfortable with. Ask survivors about their childhood before the Holocaust. Ask them to share what life was like for Jews in their town/country. Did they live in an area with only Jews? Did they go to synagogue, to religious school? How did they celebrate the Jewish holidays? Ask survivors to speak about Jewish and non-Jewish people who helped them and their families. Ask them how they got to North America. Try to film your interview to create a permanent archive to share with others.

Real Kids, Real Mitzvot

Matt G.—Sharing His Love of Reading

A book a week: Matt is a huge reader. In fact, in addition to reading books required for school, he reads at least one or two other books each week, even more in the summer. History, mystery, science fiction, and nonfiction—Matt loves them all.

Stocking a library: Matt's dad volunteers for Friends of Pine Ridge Reservation (www.friendsofpineridgereservation.org), an organization that supports the Lakota Sioux in North Dakota. Matt contacted the librarian on the Native American reservation to ask what types of books were missing from their library's collection. Matt gathered new and used books from his neighbors, friends, and classmates. He also spent a portion of the money he received as Bar Mitzvah gifts to buy additional books appropriate for the age groups most in need of reading material and resources. Hopefully, the books Matt donated are helping kids on the reservation become book lovers, too.

Brian H.—Bringing Books to Cancer Patients

First hand: Brian was nine years old when his mother went through treatments to battle breast cancer. So, for his mitzvah project, he wanted to brighten the day of kids undergoing cancer treatments. Brian wrote a letter to ask friends and relatives to donate money to buy books for kids at Boston-based Dana-Farber/Children's Hospital Cancer Center (www.danafarberchildrens.org). Obviously, his words were persuasive. Brian raised more than $600 and purchased approximately three hundred books, DVDs, and children's games.

Second nature: Brian did more than donate materials to the oncology/hematology unit at the hospital. He also donated his time and his bright smile, reading and playing with young patients as he offered each of them a chance to pick out a few books to keep.

Max M.—Books on the Beat

Talking with the chief of police: Max wanted to collect children's books to give to police officers. Why would police officers want a pile of kids' books? So they could hand them out to kids while patrolling neighborhoods. Sometimes, police visit homes to help out victims of domestic violence or other traumatic experiences. Max realized that in frightening situations like these, a book could ease a child's distress. Max met with the chief of his county's police department to present his idea, and the chief liked it!

Bags and boxes of books: Max set up a drop-off box at his school and another at his synagogue, and he collected hundreds of books. After sorting the books by age group, Max dropped the books off at the central police station for officers to have handy in their patrol cars when a book can help ease a child's fear.

Sam L.—Lending a Hand for a Lending Library

Building community: A program at Sam's synagogue and advice from his rabbi inspired Sam's mitzvah project. Sam's synagogue partners with Beyond Shelter (www.beyondshelter.org), an organization that builds and runs permanent housing for homeless families in Los Angeles. Sam contacted the director of Beyond Shelter to see how he could help. The director told Sam about a new building under construction in South L.A. for about 150 people and explained that Beyond Shelter needed help creating a children's library in the building.

Building a library: Sam collected thousands of books from friends, family, and his school community; donated money for shelves and chairs; and together with the kids who would soon be moving into the building, spent several days organizing the library. Sam explained how his appreciation for books inspired his project: "I am a big reader and a lover of books, and I wanted to base my project around literacy. Rabbi Klein told me about this place, and it turned out they needed a library. So it was a perfect fit." After his Bar Mitzvah, Sam continued his support of Beyond Shelter, including hosting a reading party at the apartment building.

Reading & Writing Journal

Put your words into action for a mitzvah project that
communicates loud and clear.

What inspired you in this chapter? Jot down ideas you want to
remember for possible mitzvah projects … and beyond.

_____

_____

_____

_____

_____

_____

_____

_____

_____

_____

_____

_____

_____

_____

_____

_____

_____

_____

_____

_____

_____

Putting Mitzvot in Motion

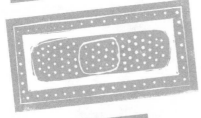

Animals

"But ask the beasts, and they will teach you; the birds of the sky, they will tell you; or speak to the earth, it will teach you; the fish of the sea, they will inform you."

—JOB 12:7–8

Train Your Dog to Do Mitzvot

If your dog is friendly to people and other dogs, then why not include him or her in your mitzvah project? Therapy Dogs International (TDI) is a volunteer organization that tests and registers dogs and owners to visit nursing homes, hospitals, schools, libraries, and anywhere else a visit from a dog will brighten someone's day. For your dog to become a therapy dog, he or she must pass a temperament evaluation, including the American Kennel Club's Canine Good Citizen Test. Accepting a friendly stranger; sitting, lying down, coming, and staying on command; and walking on a loose leash and through a crowd are a few of the commands you must teach your dog. If visiting others with your dog appeals to you, then learn more at www.tdi-dog.org. You'll need a grown-up to accompany you and your dog.

✓ Get It Going

Tail Waggin' Tutors, TDI's reading program, helps children over-come the anxiety of reading out loud by having kids read to a nonjudgmental dog. Tail Waggin' Tutors often bring their dogs to libraries and elementary schools and listen as kids read to them. Who knows, one day you and your dog may inspire a life-long reader.

Protect Endangered Species

Perhaps you have a dog, a cat, or maybe a rabbit or a guinea pig. Would you also like to have an endangered species, like a polar bear, a ring-tailed lemur, or even an orangutan for a pet? You can "adopt" an endangered species, which means donating money to support conservation efforts on their behalf. Symbolic adoptions start at around $20 and include a certificate of adoption as well as a photo of the species. You can even make adoptions in other peo-ple's names. What a wonderful way to honor a kindred animal lover.

✓ Get It Going

The World Wildlife Fund (WWF, www.worldwildlife.org) offers one hundred different species for symbolic adoption. The National Wildlife Federation (NWF, www.nwf.org) is another organization that works to protect endangered species and offers about fifteen species of baby animals to adopt. Pick a species you care to save. Make endangered species the theme for your table decorations at your Bar/Bat Mitzvah lunch or dinner. Both the WWF and the NWF sell stuffed animals and other items you could use as cen-terpieces … and then donate to kids in need.

Walk Dogs to Raise Money for Animals

To raise money for your favorite animal-related charity, why not start a dog-walking business? There are many reasons people may need your services—they could be gone from home all day, busy with work, sick, or just need a little extra help. Make sure you put up posters, send e-mails, and spread the word to friends and neighbors with dogs. Publicize your dog-walking service at local veterinarians' offices, too. Remember to communicate where you will be donating the money, as this will encourage animal lovers to hire you. Need a name for your service … what about "Paws in the Park"? Last but not least, don't forget the dog treats!

✓ Get It Going

To figure out what to charge for your services, find out what competitors in your area charge. Look online and at your veterinarian's office for other dog walkers' fees. Do they charge per walk, per hour, per half hour? Since you're not a professional, it probably makes sense to charge less.

Befriend a Feline

Do you like cats? Many Siamese, tabby, long- or short-haired cats and others are waiting to be adopted at local shelters. But without caring, human interaction, these animals can become shy and insecure. If animals waiting to be adopted as household pets are scared of people, then they are unlikely to be brought into a home. With an adult to accompany you, you can visit an animal shelter and pet cats that are in need of human company. Your visits will aid your feline friends as they become happier and friendlier!

✓ Get It Going

If you cannot travel to a shelter or you have allergies but still care greatly for cats, there are other ways to help shelters! You can volunteer to put flyers in public places like libraries or coffee shops to advertise upcoming pet adoption events. You could also tackle a spring-cleaning task: collect clean, used towels and blankets from your home and from others to give to the local shelter. Animal shelters always need them for drying off the animals and creating soft beds.

Give Animals a Voice

The Humane Society of the United States (www.humanesociety.org) is the nation's largest animal protection organization. One of the most important roles it plays is to investigate animal neglect and abuse. Humane Societies rely on people to contact them on behalf of animals. In Washington, D.C., for example, the capital's Humane Society recognized as heroes the one hundred students who had each reported a neglected animal. Give animals a voice and promote humane treatment toward animals by speaking out. Report a lost or neglected pet to the Humane Society. Write an article for your school newspaper encouraging kids to look out for animals and educating them about the Humane Society. Or make a poster or write a school report to educate others about the importance of kind treatment of animals.

✔ Get It Going

To find animal protection groups in your area, look under "animal shelters" in the phone book; search online, using your city and the words "animal shelter"; or visit www.petfinder.org. If you are having a party to celebrate your Bar/Bat Mitzvah, you could create baskets full of pet collars, pet food, and animal toys to use as centerpieces, and then donate them to an animal rescue organization after the party.

Feed Feathered Friends

Birds are critical to our environment—they reduce pests and spread seeds. Read a book about bird feeding and attracting birds to your own yard. More than one hundred North American bird species complement their natural diets with birdseed, fruit, nectar, and suet that they eat from bird feeders. Set up a bird feeder. Plant a native fruit or berry-producing bush or tree. Add a birdbath to your landscape for clean drinking and bath water for birds. You'll likely see new species stop by for some healthy fast food!

✓ Get It Going

Think about participating in the Great American Backyard Bird Count, a four-day annual event that involves bird-watchers of all ages counting birds all across the United States. "Citizen scientists" count birds for as little as fifteen minutes, or longer, over the four-day period and report their observations. Check out www.birdcount.org for how to join this effort. You might need a bird guide to help you identify all the birds you spot.

Real Kids, Real Mitzvot

Sophie B.—Socializing Pups

In Israel: Before Sophie's Bat Mitzvah, her family took a trip to Israel, where she visited several organizations and people who are making the world a better place. One of the organizations Sophie visited was the Israel Guide Dog Center for the Blind (www.israelguidedog.org), the only center of its kind in Israel. Sophie learned firsthand how the pups are trained, how matches between dogs and people are made, and she even participated in training blindfolded, with guide dogs leading her. Sophie fell in love with the Israel Guide Dog Center and invited her friends and family to make a donation to the center in honor of her Bat Mitzvah in lieu of gifts. She was very proud to raise the money to cover the cost of training thirty puppies!

Closer to home: But Sophie wanted to do more than send money. She wanted hands-on involvement in her own neighborhood. Sophie researched guide dog centers in her area and found one about an hour away from her home that trains puppies and then matches the dogs with the visually impaired. Coincidentally, this center even supplies some of the pups used in Israel! Sophie trained for the weekend socialization program and had the thrill of bringing home very young puppies to expose them to as many new smells, sounds, and situations as possible. Sophie had to follow strict rules with the puppies and found it much harder than she'd imagined. But it was lots of fun and rewarding, too!

Emily M.—No Horsing Around

Walk, trot: Emily loves horses and wanted to share her love of riding with other children for her mitzvah project. Through her friends, Emily found a therapeutic horseback riding program for kids with either behavioral issues or developmental disabilities.

Canter, gallop: Emily began volunteering for the therapeutic horseback-riding program about a year before her Bat Mitzvah and continues today, two years later. Every week she has played games with four- to ten-year-old kids while they ride horses to help them with balance, social skills, and speaking. Emily plans to continue working at the riding center throughout high school, since her work there brings happiness and physical conditioning to the kids as well as to herself.

Jesse S.—Helping Animals Help People

Service monkeys: Jesse's father had a spinal cord injury a couple of years before Jesse's Bar Mitzvah. So, in honor of his special day, Jesse identified organizations that help people with spinal cord injuries. Since his family also loved animals, Jesse chose Helping Hands: Monkey Helpers for the Disabled (www.monkeyhelpers.org) on the Internet. The organization trains and places capuchin monkeys with individuals who are paralyzed or who live with severe mobility impairments. Jesse included both a personal note in his invitations requesting donations instead of gifts and a Helping Hands brochure to introduce people to the organization. While Jesse raised almost $3,000, he hopes that because of his Bar Mitzvah many more people know about Helping Hands and will continue to support the organization.

Service dogs: As if supporting Helping Hands wasn't enough, in the year leading up to his Bar Mitzvah, Jesse and his mom attended six months of therapy dog training with his dog, Louie. Now, Jesse and Louie visit residents at a geriatric center. Louie's specialty is socializing with people with dementia. It's clear that Jesse understands how important animals are in people's lives.

Ellie L.—Fostering Kittens for the Humane Society

Loving animals: Ellie has always loved animals, so it was only natural that her mitzvah project would involve them. She talked with a local animal shelter and learned about their foster pet program. Since her family already had a dog and she wasn't interested in gerbils, guinea pigs, or rabbits, she decided to foster kittens. To foster kittens, she and her family raised the small cats in their finished basement until they were two-and-a-half pounds.

Caring for kittens: Ellie scooped the litter pan, fed the kittens, and changed their water twice a day. She gave them warm blankets and lots of tender loving care. Ellie's family typically had one to four kittens at a time, and to date, she has fostered over thirty-five kittens. Ellie explains her love for fostering kittens: "My favorite part is playing with the kittens and naming them. I also feel especially good when I get an e-mail saying that one of 'my' kittens has been adopted." Ellie also made "cat hammocks" and opened a contributions web page that has raised over $600. Ellie can't wait to become an official volunteer at the shelter when she is older and knows she will continue working there for years to come.

Julia R.—Preparing for Pet Therapy

Share the love: When it came time for Julia to figure out her mitzvah project, her new dog, Buddy, was at the front of her mind. He was a big, friendly, and gentle bundle of love. He always made her feel great. She wanted other people to be greeted by his warm eyes and enjoy petting his soft coat. Julia decided to tackle the task of going through educational training with Buddy to be certified to visit nursing homes.

Best in class: Julia and Buddy joined the Delta Society (www.deltasociety.org), a not-for-profit group that works to improve human health through service and therapy animals. In their Pet Partners program, Julia and her dog took classes, studied (well, Julia studied and Buddy practiced!), and were tested on what they had learned. Then, for the entire year of her Bat Mitzvah, Julia and Buddy visited the senior residents at a neighborhood assisted-living facility.

Sarah D. and Matthew D.—Preparing Puppies as Possible Guides

Home school: For about a year before their respective Bat and Bar Mitzvah, Sarah and her younger brother, Matthew, brought puppies into their home as part of a program with Guiding Eyes for the Blind (www.guidingeyes.org). The organization's purpose is to socialize puppies and familiarize them with family life. Guiding Eyes gave Sarah and Matthew a puppy carrying case for the car, the leashes, the food, dog toys, and a pen—they needed to supply time, patience, and lots of love!

Practice makes perfect: Sarah and Matthew hosted two or three six-week-old puppies at a time for three or four days.

The puppies would get used to all the regular noises of a busy family, including the television, vacuum cleaner, telephone, and children shouting. The brother and sister helped the puppies practice going up and down stairs and do their business outdoors. After the four days, each group of puppies went back to the organization to be evaluated for their suitability as future guide dogs. Matthew felt the hardest part was returning the puppies to the organization each time: "I really felt a special connection with Darwin, one of the puppies. And I wished he could have stayed with us, but I knew he was going to be with someone who needed him and would really love him."

Animal Journal

Noah helped the animals two by two, but you can do a
mitzvah just by helping one.

What inspired you in this chapter? Jot down ideas you want to
remember for possible mitzvah projects ... and beyond.

_____

_____

_____

_____

_____

_____

_____

_____

_____

_____

_____

_____

_____

_____

_____

_____

_____

_____

_____

_____

Camp

"Summer camp was such a meaningful and fun way for our kids to strengthen their Jewish identity. In the most relaxed and supportive atmosphere, they made lifelong friendships and connections to their heritage."

—DALE SORCHER, PARENT OF JEWISH OVERNIGHT CAMPERS

Spread the Word about Jewish Overnight Camps

Do you go to a Jewish overnight camp? Why not help spread the word to encourage more kids to attend your camp or another Jewish overnight camp that meets their needs? Not only will you help another kid have a great summer, but also you'll help strengthen the Jewish community for years to come. According to the Foundation for Jewish Camp (www.jewishcamp.org), children who attend Jewish summer camps are more likely to join a synagogue or a Jewish Community Center, support Jewish charities, and become leaders in the Jewish community.

✓ Get It Going

There are many ways to build excitement for Jewish camping. Create a flyer to hand out to kids at your temple. Share photos as well as your thoughts about why camp is fun. Or become a camp liaison! Contact your camp director and offer to speak to families considering your camp. Wouldn't you have liked to talk to a kid who goes to your camp before you made the decision to attend?

Give the Gift of Summer Camp

Wouldn't you love to help a kid who otherwise couldn't get a chance to experience the wonder of summer camp? Swimming in a lake, making new friends, singing around a campfire, celebrating Shabbat under the stars—camp experiences make memories that last a lifetime. Not to mention the unforgettable bug juice and bugs! Many camps have scholarship funds. You could decide to ask camp friends, school friends, and family to donate money to a camp fund in honor of your Bar or Bat Mitzvah. You could also make your own cash contribution.

✓ Get It Going

The Foundation for Jewish Camp builds "community by the cabinful" by giving financial support to first-time overnight campers and also encourages Russian-speaking Jews in North America to attend Jewish overnight camp. This organization offers financial and professional resources to almost 150 camps. Learn more about it at www.jewishcamp.org.

Send Supplies to Summer Camp

Can you imagine all the thousands of items a not-for-profit camp needs to keep its campers busy, happy, healthy, and safe during the summer? It takes a lot more than sunshine and spirit for a great camp experience. You can help out a not-for-profit camp that hosts campers with special needs by collecting supplies to help ease the cost of running these summer programs. Office supplies, snacks, and arts and crafts items are often on camp wish lists. They may not sounds as exciting as kayaks, but gifts of these everyday items can go a long way toward helping a kid have a fantastic time at camp.

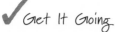 **Get It Going**

Camp Kesem was started by four students and an adult at the Hillel, a college-based Jewish community center, at Stanford University in 2001 as a way to give some "magic" to kids whose parents are coping with cancer. (*Kesem* means "magic" in Hebrew.) Camp Kesem has now expanded to more than twenty camps in fifteen states across the United States. These camps are open to any child—regardless of religion, race, or ethnicity—who has a parent with cancer. Check out www.campkesem.org to find out where you could donate needed supplies.

Introduce an Israeli Child to Camp

Do you love camp, or can you imagine how great it would be to go to camp? A fun couple of weeks away from home in a peaceful spot is a welcome break for any kid, but especially for a kid from Israel who has experienced war or terrorism. You can raise funds to provide a rejuvenating camp experience for a boy or girl who has been through a traumatic event. There are countless ways to raise money for camperships. One idea is to sell handmade camp-related items, such as camp-themed decorated laundry bags or personalized stationery and postcards. What parents don't love receiving notes from their child at camp?

✓ **Get It Going**

Here is information on restorative camping experiences for Israeli children. B'nai B'rith International began Camp Passport in 2003, bringing Israeli kids whose families have been victims of war or terrorism to the United States for a summer of camp and healing in Pennsylvania or Wisconsin. B'nai B'rith also partners with the Koby Mandell Foundation to give one hundred children evacuated from Gaza a typical camp experience in Israel. Explore www.bnaibrith.org and www.kobymandell.org to learn more about the impact of these camping programs.

Share Your Talent at a Local Camp

Do you have a special skill or hobby that you could share with younger kids at a day camp? Maybe you know some great magic tricks or you sing in your school or synagogue chorus. Do you like to dance hip-hop or break-dance? Younger kids look up to kids your age and would love to be entertained by preteens during lunch or rest period. If it is appropriate, you could even have the campers participate after you perform.

✓ Get It Going

Have your parents help you find a local Jewish Community Center or town or county program that runs summer day camps for kids with special needs or from families in need. Then call or e-mail the camp director to start exploring volunteer options for the weeks of the summer that you are home. Sharing your talents with other kids might just be the perfect way to share your camp spirit!

Welcome New Campers to Your Home Away from Home

Before you even step foot on camp soil, you can perform the mitzvah of welcoming strangers, called *hachnasat orchim*. Do you remember how you felt before you went to overnight camp for the first time? Likely you were excited and nervous at the same time—feeling like a stranger! Would you have appreciated meeting a veteran camper before heading off to camp so that you would see at least one familiar face once summer arrived?

✓ Get It Going

Call the director of your camp to find the names and contact information for kids in your town and towns nearby who will be going to your summer camp for the first time. Send them an e-mail or a text message and strike up a conversation. Tell them your favorite parts of camp. Ask them to send you questions, no matter how silly they may seem. Then, invite the kids over for a couple of hours on a weekend. Be sure to have lots of camp photos around to share. And once camp starts, offer to be a "big brother" or "big sister" to your new friends.

Real Kids, Real Mitzvot

Daniel G.—Creating Camp Spirit

Reveille: Overnight camp has always been a really big part of Daniel's life—the wilderness, the activities, the friendships, even the food. So when it came time to come up with an idea for a mitzvah project, Daniel knew it had to relate to summer camp.

Taps: With the help of his parents, Daniel found an overnight camp for kids living in the Northwest Side of Chicago, funded by the Northwestern University Settlement House (www.nush.org), an organization that helps people cope with the obstacles of poverty. Daniel contacted the camp to see how he could help and learned that the camp needed sports equipment. Together with his friends, Daniel collected new and used baseball bats, lacrosse sticks, basketballs, and more. To complete the list of requested equipment, Daniel used money he received for his Bar Mitzvah. He wanted to be sure that all campers had the equipment they needed to enjoy sports ... and camp.

Allie H. and Rachel H.—Yard Sale for Camp

Nature calls: Allie and Rachel were friends at music camp in Maine and wanted to give the camp experience to kids whose families could not afford to send them to sleepaway camp. The girls decided to host a yard sale to raise money for the

Washington Post fund that sends at-risk kids from Washington, D.C., to Camp Moss Hollow (www.familymattersdc.org).

Calls answered: After asking neighbors for items to sell at their yard sale, great stuff appeared in their driveways. Neighbors cleaned out their garages and basements, sent over long-forgotten wedding gifts, and donated many out-grown and unwanted items. The girls spent hours making and putting up posters in the neighborhood, cleaning and tagging the items, and then staffing the yard sale. In addition to learning about the beauty of giving, Allie and Rachel learned about how mitzvot beget other mitzvot. The boys next door saw a great opportunity to make money with a car wash when they noticed all the cars lining the street. The brothers earned so much money that they donated a portion of their bounty to Allie and Rachel's cause.

Alexa S.—Dance-a-thon Camp-a-thon

Let's dance: For her mitzvah project, Alexa S. hosted a dance-a-thon for middle school students at her synagogue. She wanted to raise money for the Israeli Neve Eliyahu Integrated Nursery School Subsidy Program. The proceeds from the dance were used to send Ethiopian children to school and summer camp. The event was held just before Rosh Hashanah, so some called it a New Year's dance. Alexa's brother inspired her to think of her dance-a-thon project: "Dan volunteered at an Israeli community center that helps needy Ethiopian Jews. I wanted to do something to help these kids, too!"

Dancing for a cause: Alexa's synagogue donated its social hall for the party. A DJ discounted his services. Friends and students from Alexa's public school and religious school got sponsors for them to dance. Each kid also made an $18 donation to participate in the dance-a-thon. Some adult friends of Alexa's family donated gifts to motivate kids to find sponsors. The kids who raised the most money won tickets to a professional baseball game and a Bruce Springsteen rock concert!

Brennan F.—Speaking Out for Kids with Epilepsy

Firsthand knowledge: Brennan's mom believes his mitzvah project found him. When he was eight, Brennan had surgery to remove a brain tumor and was also diagnosed with epilepsy. He and his family have faced these challenges with the support of the Epilepsy Foundation of Arizona (EFAz, www.epilepsyfoundation.org/arizona). Brennan really enjoyed his weeklong summer stays at EFAz's Camp Candlelight, with canoeing, paintball, campfires, as well as sessions that teach about seizures. Not surprisingly, Brennan chose to support EFAz and to be an advocate for epilepsy issues for his mitzvah project.

Speaking from the heart: Brennan raised money for the organization by participating in Phoenix's Epilepsy Walk. He also represented his state as part of the National Epilepsy Foundation's "Kids Speak Up Program" (www.epilepsyfoundation.org/ksu). Through that group, he went to Washington, D.C., and discussed epilepsy with both of his U.S. senators and members of Congress. He also spoke on Radio Disney about his experience and how much he enjoyed Camp Candlelight. Brennan's Bar Mitzvah haftarah portion (2 Kings 4:1–37) related so closely to his personal experience that it seemed chosen especially for him. In this portion, a boy collapses in a field as he calls out, "Oh, my head, my head!" (2 Kings 4:19). What an incredible coincidence that Brennan's Bar Mitzvah was on his birthday weekend and the fourth anniversary of his surgery.

Camp Journal

Bonfires, s'mores, sailing, archery ... share the spirit of camp!

What inspired you in this chapter? Jot down ideas you want to remember for possible mitzvah projects ... and beyond.

Fitness

"Blessed are You, Eternal our God, Source of the
universe, who with wisdom formed the human body...."
—TALMUD, BERACHOT 60B

Plan a "Shabbat" Get Outdoors Day

In 2008, the U.S. Forest Service and the American Recreation Coalition (www.funoutdoors.com) launched an annual Get Outdoors Day event in June to encourage healthy, active fun in nature. You can follow this good example and organize a Shabbat Get Outdoors Day for kids in your temple. Plan a snack in the park, an outdoor sing-along, and a nature craft to entertain the kids.

✔ Get It Going

Here's an idea for turning a craft into a snack. Have the kids create edible "ants on a log." All you need are celery sticks for the log, with peanut butter or cream cheese spread on top, and raisins for the ants crawling up. Or create edible ladybugs with red grapes cut in half for the head and hulled strawberries with mini chocolate chips pressed in the berries for the bodies—all skewered on a toothpick to hold the ladybug together.

Clean Up a Local Playground or Park

Yard work is good exercise. Raking and bagging leaves, weeding flower beds, and picking up trash all get your heart pumping, your muscles moving, and your spirit soaring. Pull together a group of friends to help you clean up a park or playground. Perhaps it is your school playground or maybe a park in a nearby town that could use some sprucing up. Coordinate with a principal or a town parks and recreation department employee before you ask friends to join you.

✓ Get It Going

Remember to have your friends bring tools and supplies needed for the cleanup: rakes, leaf and garbage bags, shovels, trowels, gardening gloves, bulbs, and plants. To keep everyone hustling and smiling, bring along a CD player or radio to blast upbeat music, and a water jug, cups, and snacks to keep everyone fueled. You could even organize contests and give prizes for the person who collects the most trash, plants the most flower bulbs, or rakes the biggest pile of leaves.

Spread Calm with Yoga

Yoga, an ancient practice that originated in India, helps people develop healthy bodies and minds. Today, people of all ages practice yoga to become limber, strong, and peaceful. If you are one of these people, organize a yoga class or a series of classes to raise money for a mental health charity. Ask your yoga teacher if he/she will donate his/her services. In addition to doing a good deed, leading your class is a good way to meet prospective students. If the teacher cannot afford to volunteer his/her services, pay the teacher yourself out of money you earn or receive for your Bar/Bat Mitzvah. Ask your parents to advance you the cash if need be. Invite friends, neighbors, and classmates and explain in your materials where you will be donating the money as well as the necessary logistics of date, time, location, and fee.

✔ Get It Going

Perhaps the best place to start to find mental health services you can support is locally. Is there a local clinic for adolescents or a teen depression prevention program in your community? Speak to your school guidance counselor or your pediatrician to locate an organization doing good work.

Plant a Flower Garden

Gardening is good for the soul as well as for the body. When you plant flowers, you beautify the world, connect to Mother Earth, and get exercise. A flower garden also lifts others' spirits. Think about who might appreciate the sight of colorful blooms as you plan where to plant a garden. How about residents at a retirement home or a senior center? What about guests at a homeless shelter or a community center? Have you considered children at a day care or after-school program? It is more than likely that whomever you approach will be thrilled by your offer to plant window boxes or an in-ground garden, depending on the available space.

✔ Get It Going

Be sure to prepare the soil before you plant. Take out rocks and weeds, aerate the soil, and spread nutrient-rich soil. Make sure to select flowers that will thrive in your climate and that are hardy, requiring little care. Consider planting perennials, flowers that bloom year after year. Besides planting the garden, return to water and weed to ensure that your garden thrives.

Help Other Kids Get and Stay Fit

Have you heard about the Presidential Active Lifestyle Award (PALA) challenge? It is a program of the President's Council on Fitness, Sports and Nutrition (www.fitness.gov), designed to help people add activity to their daily lives and reward them when they do. It's a mitzvah to help others stay fit, and it's easier to get fit if you're working with others. So why not organize a PALA group for kids your age? To get started, learn about the challenge and promote your idea of forming a group of kids with a common fitness goal. Next, plan to meet a couple of times a week—such as an early school release day and a weekend day—to exercise as a group. Last but not least, lead the group toward your collective goal.

✓ Get It Going

For kids and teens between six and seventeen years old, the PALA challenge requires physical activity sixty minutes a day, at least five days a week, for six out of eight weeks. To learn all the details, go to www.presidentschallenge.org. You can even buy official certificates, emblems, magnets, T-shirts, hats, and more to reward your team once you've reached your target.

Organize Walk-to-School Days

How do you typically get to and from school? Do you take the bus or get a ride from your parents or neighbors when you could safely walk instead? Walking is good not only for health, but also for the environment. So reduce your carbon footprint and increase your footsteps by organizing walk-to-school days on a weekly, monthly, or bimonthly schedule after discussing safety with your parent(s).

✓ Get It Going

You could organize walk-to-school days for kids in your neighborhood or school-wide. If school-wide participation is your goal, then approach your principal with the idea. If she or he is on board, announce the walk-to-school days in your school newsletter, with posters on the school bulletin boards, over the PA system, and through e-mail. Make sure to promote the health and environmental benefits to encourage participation. Maybe you can get a local supermarket to donate energy bars to have at the entrance to school for everyone who walks. And always put safety first.

Real Kids, Real Mitzvot

Rose G.—Turning Her Party into a Fitness Project

A new way to party: When it came time to plan Rose's Bat Mitzvah, Rose and her parents wanted the entire celebration to reflect their values. So, in place of a traditional dance party for the kids, they offered Rose's friends a fun day of community service. Rose's mom contacted Chicago Cares (www.chicagocares.org), an organization that coordinates community service projects in and around Chicago, to help her plan a service opportunity that fit with Rose's passion for running.

The invitation says it all: "Rose loves to run fast. Please join her in a community service project to mark her milestone and feed her passion. We'll refurbish a school, encourage their track program, and have fun. Lunch served. Dress for a mess." At Rose's party, instead of dancing to the music blasting from the sound system, she and her friends painted walls and cleaned up the outdoor track area at a public school where 95 percent of the kids come from low-income households. What a way to move to the music!

Ben R.—Soccer 4 Haiti

Shared pastime: Ben loves soccer almost as much as do the kids in the Caribbean islands. When a devastating earthquake hit Haiti, the poorest country in the Western Hemisphere, international aid focused on lifesaving support such as food, medicine, and shelter. After Ben's friend's dad, an emergency room doctor, came back from assisting in Haiti, Ben and his friends came up with the idea of giving Haitian kids something fun to do as their country regrouped from destruction. They started an organization called Soccer 4 Haiti (www.soccer4haiti.org) and collected new and used soccer balls to send to Haitian boys and girls.

Winning goal: For his mitzvah project, Ben participated in a sixty-two-mile bike ride and raised $2,000 to purchase soccer balls for Haitian kids, made by widows in Afghanistan who hand-sew them in their homes. These widows are participants in Beyond the 11th (www.beyondthe11th.org), a nonprofit organization that provides support to widows in Afghanistan who have been afflicted by war, terrorism, and oppression. Ben's mother started Beyond the 11th after losing her husband and Ben's dad, on September 11, 2001. Ben and his mom are both determined to make the world a better place.

Alex H.—Swimming for a Cure

Doing laps: Alex has been an avid swimmer since he was eight years old. So it was a natural choice for him to decide to raise money to help others by swimming. Alex asked people to "sponsor" his big swims with local swim clubs. For each big swim, a sponsor would make a donation. Alex started his mitzvah project a few years before he turned thirteen. That enabled him to raise even more money for his charities of choice, the National Multiple Sclerosis Society (www.nationalmssociety.org) and Swim Across America (www.swimacrossamerica.org), which raises money for cancer research.

Making waves: By age sixteen, Alex had swum the three miles across the Hudson River in New York four times and the Long Island Sound twice. In total, through donations from family, friends, and strangers, Alex has raised nearly $30,000 for his chosen charities. For Alex, swimming is hard work and rewarding, and now also a way to give to others. He believes, "We should not take our good health for granted!"

Sam H.—Hosting a Game-a-thon

Play for a cause: Sam wanted to help the Dystonia Medical Research Foundation (DMRF, www.dystonia-foundation.org), a group dedicated to researching cures and providing support for people with the neurological movement disorder that causes muscles to contract and spasm involuntarily. Dystonia sometimes has a genetic basis that affects Jews of Ashkenazi descent—that is, descendants of Jews from Eastern and Central Europe—including Sam's uncle. Sam sister's school raised money with a jog-a-thon. He changed the concept into a game-a-thon for his friends. Sam promoted the game-a-thon with flyers around his temple. He also made an announcement at Friday night services. His classmates and friends joined in for six hours of games on a Sunday right after Hebrew school in his synagogue's social hall. The kids asked people to sponsor them with donations for each hour they played games.

Fun for funds: All the kids had a blast exercising and playing Twister, DanceDanceRevolution, and board and video games while they raised money for DMRF. Sam's family supplied snacks and served frozen pizzas, which they heated in the synagogue's kitchen. Sam said, "This project raised awareness about dystonia but also brought kids together at temple for a fun time and a good cause." A few months after the event, Sam's mom got a call from DMRF. They asked "if she realized he had raised $1,800—*chai* times 100." What a symbolic coincidence! (The word "life" in Hebrew is *chai*, and the numerical value of *chai* equals eighteen. Money in multiples of eighteen are frequently given as gifts at Jewish life-cycle events.)

Fitness Journal

Get up and get going to make your mark on the world.

What inspired you in this chapter? Jot down ideas you want to remember for possible mitzvah projects ... and beyond.

_____

_____

_____

_____

_____

_____

_____

_____

_____

_____

_____

_____

_____

_____

_____

_____

_____

_____

_____

_____

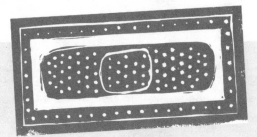

Health

"Hope lies in dreams, in imagination, and in the courage of those who dare to make dreams into reality."
—JONAS SALK (1914–1995), POLIO VACCINE CREATOR

Organize a Blood Drive or Bone Marrow Donation Registration at Your Temple

Does your temple hold a blood or bone marrow registration drive? Giving blood or bone marrow is truly giving the gift of life. Many lifesaving medical treatments require blood transfusions, and for many types of blood cancers and disorders, a bone marrow transplant is a patient's only chance for survival. As a preteen or young teen, you are not old enough to donate either blood or bone marrow. But you could suggest that your temple host a drive and help organize an event with adult assistance. Your advocacy and your hard work will save lives—the ultimate mitzvah. The mitzvah of saving a life is called *pikuach nefesh*.

✔ Get It Going

To learn about organizing an event, go to Gift of Life Bone Marrow Foundation (www.giftoflife.org) and the American Red Cross (www.redcrossblood.org). At a blood drive, donors actually give blood. At a bone marrow registration drive, donors only get a simple cheek swab to determine if they match someone in need.

Help Find a Cure for Tay-Sachs

Tay-Sachs is a genetic disease that causes a deterioration of mental and physical abilities, typically starting around six months of age and usually resulting in death by the age of four. You may not have heard of Tay-Sachs because the disease is rare, but there is no cure or treatment. Sometimes referred to as a Jewish disease, the disease is prominent among Ashkenazim, descendants of Jews from Eastern and Central Europe, but also in French Canadians of southeastern Quebec, and Cajuns of southern Louisiana. There are many ways you can raise money, but one is to reach out to families with healthy little children. Create a flyer about the disease and why you think it important to find a cure. Then distribute the flyer with an envelope for contributions. Of course, you can also e-mail the flyer with instructions for how to contribute. Offer parents the opportunity to make their contribution in honor of their healthy children to bring home the message of how fortunate they are.

✓ Get It Going

To learn more, go to www.ntsad.org, the website of the National Tay-Sachs & Allied Diseases Association.

Help Seniors Exercise Their Brains

A portion of age-related memory loss comes from a lack of mental exercise and stimulation. You can help elders prevent cognitive decline by playing word games, carrying on conversations, and watching movies or TV together and then talking about what you saw. Contact the program director at a local senior center, retirement community, or assisted-living residence to see if you can visit with a group or a single person. Agree to times and dates when you are available.

✓ Get It Going

Not sure what type of games to play with seniors? Bingo,
Scrabble, Apples to Apples, and charades are all good choices.
You could also bring coffee-table-type books to share and discuss.
Perhaps your family has a book of paintings or of photographs
that would spark interesting conversation.

Conquer Cancer

Cancer is the general name for a group of more than one hundred
diseases in which cells in a part of the body begin to grow out of
control. There are so very many ways you can help conquer cancer.
You could raise money to donate for research to develop cures or
to help pay for the nonmedical expenses—such as rent payments,
day care, and housekeeping—of cancer patients who are unable to
work outside or inside the home. You could provide entertainment
for children who are undergoing cancer treatment, such as art
projects, books, and music. You could cook food for a family with
a member who has cancer. The list goes on and on.

✓ Get It Going

Would you like to help out a family in your town who has a family member with cancer? Prepare a variety of meals that can be
frozen so healthy food is always close at hand. Make sure to put
the meals in containers that go in the freezer and that you do
not need returned to you. Label each one with ingredients just
in case the family has food allergies or aversions, and include
heating instructions, too.

Provide Fresh Produce to a Food Bank

Most of the food people donate to a food bank is canned or boxed.
While fresh fruits and vegetables are so healthful, they are also per-
ishable and expensive. But people in need would surely enjoy and
benefit from more fresh produce. Consider organizing a food

drive at a farmers' market. You can ask shoppers to buy a little extra to donate to hungry members of the community. Maybe even the farmers will decide to help your cause, too!

✓ Get It Going

First, check with your local food bank to find out what fresh food they accept and when. Then contact the organizer of a local farmers' market and ask if you can collect donations for a food pantry at the market. If the answer is yes, make signs explaining your project, and set them up in a designated area. Bring along boxes and bags to collect the bounty, and enlist a few grown-ups to drive you to the food bank to deliver the fresh produce. Hopefully, you'll need a driver with a minivan to transport lots of fresh fruits and veggies! And don't give up if you can't coordinate with a farmers' market! Another way to gather lots of fresh fruit and vegetables is to organize a group to go to a pick-your-own farm. Apples, pears, beans, peas, berries, and squash are all fun to pick and delicious to eat. Maybe you and your friends will inspire the pick-your-own farm to donate, as well.

Send Inspirational Notes

Do you find that a simple phrase or a few words can help you see things in a whole new way? Meaningful thoughts often motivate people to think differently, overcome fear, appreciate what they have, believe in themselves, and reach out to help others. Collect inspirational sayings to give to people whose spirit needs a lift. It could be a friend who has moved to a new city, a teammate who has broken a bone, or a friend whose relative has passed away. Write the inspirational sayings out by hand on beautiful paper, or surround them with drawings. Make it a goal to give out at least four quotes a month to be sure to spread inspiration all around.

✓ Get It Going

Write your own original inspirational thoughts and quotes from famous people past and present. There are books and websites full of inspirational quotes. You'll definitely get inspired yourself from others' words of wisdom, too.

Real Kids, Real Mitzvot

Nine 7th Graders—Teens Helping Teens Cope

Reaching out: For their group mitzvah project, nine 7th graders reached out to other teens whose parents were in the hospital with cancer. They understood that families of cancer patients had it tough, too.

Packing up: The teens packed gym bags with fleece blankets, Boston Red Sox caps, mechanical pens, Mad Libs, a deck of cards, a journal, and other items. "We chose things kids could use while they were at the hospital to help get their minds off their parents having cancer," one student explained. The students approached a local sports company, Reebok, to donate the gym bags, and the students raised money for the contents through bake sales. Yes, cookies and brownies can be put to good use!

Rachel H.—Reaching Out to Others with Crohn's Disease

Up close: Rachel has Crohn's disease, so for her mitzvah project she decided to support an organization that is relevant to her, the Crohn's & Colitis Foundation of America (CCFA, www.ccfa.org). Rachel volunteered several days in their local office and spent much of her time providing administrative support for the CCFA annual fund-raising walk that begins on Boston Common.

And personal: Two years in a row, Rachel walked the CCFA walk herself, raising funds for the organization. In addition, during the spring and fall before her Bat Mitzvah, Rachel set up a table in the lobby of her synagogue and sold "Got Guts" rubber bracelets to raise additional funds for CCFA.

Harrison H. and Devon H.—Hospital Holiday Toy Drive

Shared experience: Harrison, Devon, another sibling, and their father all have the same bone disease, called multiple hereditary exostosis, or bumpy bone disease. Their condition requires them to visit a special doctor twice a year and undergo surgeries. Harrison and Devon both knew that kids undergoing these treatments could use a boost of happiness at holiday time.

Shared spirit: The brother and sister collected new toys, clothing, and gift cards for the children at the hospital over the holidays. Because many of the patients come from impoverished areas, the holiday party at the hospital is often the only celebration the children attend. Through e-mail requests to friends, family, and their school communities, the siblings collected enough gifts to give one to each and every child at the party.

Leah P.—A Backyard Carnival for Muscular Dystrophy Association

From a small acorn: Leah's mitzvah project was an easy choice for her—she would host a backyard carnival for the Muscular Dystrophy Association (MDA, www.mdausa.org), just as she has done since she was six years old. Back then, knowing her parents had chaired several events for MDA, Leah asked her mom how she could help, too. Together, they planned a small, homey, fun charity event, with games from their closet, like "Twister," and recycled prizes from restaurant giveaways and birthday party favors. She and her mom baked lots of brownies to pass out as treats. A few dozen of her friends came and donated money to attend. It was a great time and a great success. Over the years, this small idea became big.

An oak tree grows: Leah started asking stores for donations of prizes, pizza, water, popcorn, fruit juice, and more for her carnival. Her parents paid for her to print flyers to advertise the carnival at her school and at her brother's preschool. The admission price was "pay what you want." Because of these efforts, attendance blossomed. Over 350 people attended Leah's last carnival! About twenty of her friends volunteered to staff the booths, sell refreshments, and help set up and clean up the yard. Leah and her friends raised many thousands of dollars for MDA—and lots of spirits, as well.

Emily S.—Assisting Seniors with Alzheimer's

Sharing Time: Emily signed up with the "Smile for Seniors Program" after she learned about it from the Jewish Community Center MetroWest Mitzvah Fair. Representatives of the fair helped Emily find a local nursing home where she could play games, do arts and crafts, or just chat with residents.

Spreading cheer: Emily visited an Alzheimer's unit whose residents have varying degrees of memory loss. Because these seniors cannot leave to visit others, Emily's time with them made a big impact. Drawing, playing bingo, and assembling puzzles with the seniors provided them with enjoyment and practice of fine motor skills, as well. Although many residents were not able to remember Emily from visit to visit, Emily's time at the nursing home was often the highlight of their day. In fact, sometimes Emily was the only visitor they had for days. One of the few Jewish women in the Alzheimer's unit became so excited whenever she saw Emily that she greeted her with, "Hello, pretty,

pretty Jewish girl!" Rather than embarrass Emily, Emily explained, "It makes me feel so happy that I can bring others so much happiness with a simple visit." Emily has continued her trips to the nursing home well past her Bat Mitzvah and plans to visit for many years to come.

Health Journal

The tools to maintain a healthy mind, body, and soul
are all precious gifts to share with others.

What inspired you in this chapter? Jot down ideas you want to
remember for possible mitzvah projects … and beyond.

_____

_____

_____

_____

_____

_____

_____

_____

_____

_____

_____

_____

_____

_____

_____

_____

_____

_____

_____

_____

Music & Dance

"Sing out from your hearts, O sing praises to God."

—DEBBIE FRIEDMAN (1951–2011), AMERICAN COMPOSER
AND SINGER OF JEWISH MUSIC

Create Custom CDs

What songs do you listen to when you need to get pumped up? How about when you need to relax? Create two different collections of your favorite songs to share with others who may need encouragement and/or serenity. Be sure to consider all genres of music—pop, rock, classical, jazz, rap, and country. And make sure the songs flow one to another. Then, burn your CDs. Make a cover for the CD case with a title for the collection. Also list the tunes and consider offering a personal message about each song or the entire collection.

✓ Get It Going

Who can you give your CDs to? How about teens undergoing cancer treatments or hospitalized for an extended period? Contact a volunteer or activities coordinator at a local hospital to find out how you can bring some musical cheer to others.

Learn to Blow the Shofar

For many people, hearing the sound of the shofar in synagogue during Rosh Hashanah and Yom Kippur is a highlight of the services. The expert who blows the ram's horn is called the *tokea* (blaster) or *ba'al tekiah* (master of the blast). It's not easy to do, but if you have big lungs and a big commitment to practice, you can carry on this ancient tradition.

✔ Get It Going

On Rosh Hashanah you hear three distinct sounds from the shofar: *tekiah*—one long, straight blast; *shevarim*—three medium wailing sounds; and *teruah*—nine fast blasts, one after the other. You'll need to learn all three to one day have the honor of blowing the shofar in synagogue.

Hold a Community Concert

Have you heard the saying "Music is the universal language"? Music unites people of all ages and interests. Can you play the piano? Sing a capella? Do you know a few friends who can strum a guitar or get feet tapping with clarinet tunes? Why not host a neighborhood concert to give kids and adults a chance to relax and enjoy each other's company. Bringing neighbors together for entertainment is a great way to help create positive community spirit.

✔ Get It Going

Look for a convenient location for your concert. Do you have a big family room? Do you have a neighbor with a large finished basement? What about an outdoor summer get-together under the stars? If you want to turn your event into a fund-raiser for a charitable organization, you could charge admission or sell CDs or snacks.

Host a Dance-a-thon

Do you and your friends love to move to the music? While some people walk or run for a cause, you can dance for one. Organize a dance-a-thon at your house or local community center one weekend afternoon or evening. Ask friends to join you and collect pledges for charity. Provide your fellow dancers with a couple of paragraphs explaining the charity for which you are raising funds. Also provide a sheet for friends to keep track of pledges and a sample thank-you note for them to give to people who pledge.

✔ Get It Going

It's all about the music. To keep your friends dancing, make sure you play tunes that keep them on their feet. Pull together dance songs on your MP3 player. Ask friends for their favorites, and check online for top dance songs from today and from the past. Cold water and energy bars will fuel the fun.

Lead Sing-alongs at Senior Centers

If music lifts your spirits, imagine the joy you could bring to elders by leading sing-alongs at senior centers. It is likely a good idea to find a musical friend or two to join you for this mitzvah project. Think about performing some of the songs and encouraging seniors to join in on others. Be sure to pick songs seniors enjoy listening to as well as familiar tunes for them to sing with you.

✔ Get It Going

Once you have located the senior centers in your area, contact their activities directors to see if they would be interested in musical performances and/or sing-alongs for their residents. If yes, inquire about the needs and capabilities of the residents. Important questions include: Would they be able to hold and read sheets with words to familiar songs like "Take Me Out to the Ballgame"? What are their favorite types of music? How long would they like to participate? Is there a piano for accompaniment? Offer to bring refreshments!

Teach Israeli Folk Dance

Israeli folk dances were created to help people of all ages from all different cultures celebrate the spirit of their new country, Israel. You can unite people young and old to celebrate the spirit of your community by hosting an Israeli folk dance at a local recreation center or at your synagogue. How about a grandparent/grandchild or parent/child folk dance session? Find a few different folk songs to dance to, and bring along recordings or find live musicians. You'll also need to get the word out and bring in refreshments to keep everyone energized!

✓ Get It Going

The hora is the most well-known Israeli folk dance and actually predates the founding of the State of Israel. While this circle dance is most often danced to the music of *Hava Nagila*, other times it is danced to klezmer music and different Israeli folk songs. Since it is the most common dance at Jewish weddings and Bar/Bat Mitzvah celebrations, it is a great one to teach and practice to different tunes.

Real Kids, Real Mitzvot

Jake L.—Bringing Music to Appalachia

Hitting a high note: When Jake and his family participated in Mitzvah Day at his temple, Jake learned about a middle school in Appalachia that needed instruments to form a school band. Given Jake's love of music, collecting instruments was a perfect project.

Striking up the band: Jake put up flyers at the temple and the schools around town asking for donations of instruments kids no longer used. In addition, Jake and his mom worked out a deal with a musical instrument rental company to purchase used instruments at a discount. He donated a portion of the money he received for his Bar Mitzvah to buy the additional instruments. Thanks to Jake, kids in Appalachia are now playing the flute, clarinet, cymbals, guitar, and trumpet!

Francine K.—Making Klezmer Music

A new tune: Francine loves to play the clarinet, so sharing her love of music with elders was a natural choice for her mitzvah project. Instead of performing tunes she already knew, Francine learned to play klezmer music, a genre popular with many elder Yiddish-speaking Jews.

An old favorite: After putting in substantial time practicing klezmer songs, Francine entertained Jewish nursing home residents with a style of music that likely brought back happy memories of celebrations and festivities. Judging from the faces of her audience, Francine knew she had brightened the elders' day. And that brightened her own!

Mallory F., Sasha B., Elizabeth Z., Sarah Z., Hanna S., Sara C., Debbie A., and Stephanie F.— Spunky Singers for Seniors

Singing brings smiles: Mallory F. enlisted her friends to get her mitzvah project up and humming. These seven seventh-grade girls and one younger sister combined something they love to do—singing—with helping others. The girls performed at senior residences in their suburban Maryland town, singing classic melodies and show tunes—the types of music kids and seniors both like.

Spontaneous sing-alongs: Before each piece, the girls took turns introducing the composer or how the song became popular. Mallory explained, "Seeing the seniors' faces light up and join in when we sang familiar tunes like 'This Land Is Your Land' reminded us that we were doing a good deed."

Max B.—Concert for a Cause

Partying with a purpose: Instead of having a party, Max celebrated his Bar Mitzvah with a Sunday afternoon benefit rock concert. His family hired three rock bands and rented a local concert hall to host the event. They donated all the funds they collected at the concert to the Interfaith Neighbors Youth Corps (www.interfaithneighbors.org), a group that engages young adults in community service projects and offers job skills training.

Rocking on: Family and friends donated to the concert instead of giving Max gifts. The general public was also invited to attend at $18 a ticket. Max advertised the concert in the newspaper and through school. Max felt he could handle not getting any presents: "Believe me, I would like presents, but I don't think I *need* them, so I thought we could give the funds to people who could really use them." The Interfaith Neighbors Youth Corps refurbished a brand-new conference room outfitted with computers with the thousands of dollars they received from Max's mitzvah project. They call the new room "The Max."

Music & Dance Journal

Did you know that *Hava Nagila* means "Let's Rejoice"? So use your love of music or dance to help others rejoice, too.

What inspired you in this chapter? Jot down ideas you want to remember for possible mitzvah projects … and beyond.

_____

_____

_____

_____

_____

_____

_____

_____

_____

_____

_____

_____

_____

_____

_____

_____

_____

_____

_____

Sports

"If you fail to prepare, you're prepared to fail."
—MARK SPITZ, OLYMPIC GOLD MEDAL SWIMMER

On Your Mark, Get Set, Go ... to Raise Funds

If you like to be active, there are many races, walks, and bicycle rides you can participate in to raise money for a charitable cause. Find out about events in your area by speaking to staff at sporting goods stores, grown-ups involved with charities you are interested in, your parents, and gym teachers. You've likely heard about national events, like the American Cancer Society's Relay for Life (www.relayforlife.org) and the Susan B. Komen Race for a Cure (www.komen.org), but there are many regional and local events as well. Once you pick a walk, run, or bike ride, get as many people as you can to sponsor you so you can raise as much money as possible.

✓ Get It Going

Training appropriately for a walk, run, or ride is important to avoid injury. Set up a training schedule with the help of a coach or experienced adult. Ask a friend or relative to join you. If you can find a training partner, all the better to keep you motivated and in good company.

Organize a Clinic

What's your favorite sport? Whether it is softball, baseball, basketball, soccer, track, or tennis, host an after-school or weekend sports clinic at a local park or schoolyard for kids in your area to raise money for any charity that you would like to support. Get friends to join you as coaches, and grown-ups to supervise, as you teach kids your secrets for shooting baskets from the free throw line, setting up soccer passes, or catching fly balls.

✓ Get It Going

How can you get the word out? Create a flyer and an e-mail explaining your clinic, the charity you are supporting, the age range of kids you are looking for, date and time, fee, and e-mail address or phone number for registering. Ask the principal at your former elementary school if school officials can distribute the flyer to kids in the appropriate grades. Get your e-mail out to neighbors and friends. Talk it up. The best marketing is word of mouth.

Support the Special Olympics

The Special Olympics (www.specialolympics.org) for athletes with intellectual disabilities was started by Eunice Kennedy Shriver in 1968, only seven weeks after her younger brother Robert was killed in Los Angeles, California, while campaigning for president of the United States. At the first Special Olympics event, fewer than 100 spectators watched 1,000 athletes from 26 states and Canada march in the opening ceremonies. Today, almost 3.5 million Special Olympic athletes train year-round in all 50 states and 170 countries. You can raise money to support the Special Olympics, or volunteer to support athlete training and competition.

✓ Get It Going

Read the Special Olympics oath below to get inspired by the spirit of the games:

> *Let me win,*
> *but if I cannot win*
> *let me be brave*
> *in the attempt.*

To find Special Olympics opportunities near where you live, go to www.specialolympics.org/program_locator.aspx.

Buy Equipment with Each of Your Goals, Baskets, RBIs...

No matter what competitive sport you enjoy, you can earn money when you play so other kids have the equipment to participate in sports, too. Organize a pledge drive. Ask relatives, family friends, and neighbors to pledge a dollar amount for each goal, basket, run batted in, or ace you make in a specified season to donate to a charity that get sports equipment to kids in need. At the end of the season, tally up your score, get the word out to all who pledged, and collect on your success.

✓ Get It Going

There are many charities that provide sports equipment for kids locally, nationally and even in other countries. For example, the National Alliance for Youth Sports (NAYS, www.nays.org) provides underprivileged youth across the world with new and gently used sports equipment through its charitable initiative, the Global Gear Drive. Good Sports (www.goodsports.org) distributes sports equipment, footwear, and apparel to community organizations offering programs to disadvantaged youth.

Share the Gift of Teamwork, Physical Achievement, and Goal Setting

If you play a sport, you understand how great it feels to work hard to achieve your personal goals. There are various athletic programs that serve kids who wouldn't otherwise have a chance to experience the joy of either team or individual sports—including kids without the means to participate, with medical conditions, or with disabilities. Engage your team in raising money for a youth sports charity. Organize good old-fashioned car washes, bake sales, recyclable bottle pick-up drives, or any other fund-raising ideas your team comes up with.

✓ Get It Going

Here are just a few organizations to introduce you to the range that supports youth sports. Tenacity (www.tenacity.org) is a tennis and academic support program for inner-city youth in Boston that serves kids after school and in the summer. A Sporting Chance (www.asportingchance.net) offers youth in Missouri who are disadvantaged, abused, or neglected programs in basketball, track, softball, volleyball, and bowling. Hodia Idaho Diabetes Youth Programs (www.hodia.org) offer a ski camp for teens between the ages of twelve and eighteen with diabetes. Now, it is your turn to find an organization that serves kids in your area or that gives kids the chance to play your favorite sport!

Send Along Stinky Sneakers

Did you know that old, smelly sneakers can one day be made into basketball and tennis courts, athletic fields, and running tracks? There are a number of recycling centers, such as Nike's Reuse-A-Shoe program, that need old athletic shoes for exactly that purpose. Collect used pairs from your neighbors, friends, synagogue families, and relatives. Search on your computer for Nike Reuse-A-Shoe (www.nikereuseashoe.com) to find a drop-off location in your area.

✔ *Get It Going*

Send e-mails to your relatives, friends, and neighbors. Create posters to hang at local supermarkets, churches, temples, libraries, and doctors' offices. Does your town have a newspaper, radio station, or cable TV show that issues public service notices for free? Can you make an announcement over your school's PA system? However you decide to communicate, remember to include the dates and location for sneaker drop-off.

Real Kids, Real Mitzvot

Ethan B.—Serving Kids with Autism

Tennis ace: Ethan loves to play tennis. For his mitzvah project, he looked for a way to use tennis to help other kids. Ethan and his mom did some research and found an organization called ACEing Autism (www.aceingautism.com), which provides tennis lessons to kids with autism.

Friend ace: Every Sunday, Ethan played tennis with seven-to fourteen-year-olds in the ACEing Autism program. Ethan loved helping kids learn how to hit the ball. But what he liked best were the bonds he made with the kids. Ethan felt special that one boy who asked everyone else in the program their names each time he saw them, always remembered Ethan's name. He also appreciated the hugs he got from kids each week.

Zach K.—SCORE for the Cure

Getting an "A": Zach's mitzvah project grew out of a challenging assignment from his fourth-grade teacher. The kids were asked to think of an idea for a charity that had an acronym—a word formed from the first letters of other words. Zach created SCORE: **S**upport **C**ancer **O**utreach **R**esearch and **E**ducation. Zach realized kids could use their passion for sports to give to others. He suggested that kids who play sports could each pledge a certain coin or dollar amount for each point their team scored during a specified game. The money collected at that game would go to children's cancer charities.

Making his mark: For his Bar Mitzvah project, Zach's parents helped him make his idea for a charity to support kids with cancer a reality. They hired a lawyer to create a not-for-profit organization—SCORE. They also partnered with a T-shirt company. Zach sold T-shirts with the phrase "Life is tough ... but so am I" at local town sports games to raise money for SCORE. Zach believes, "SCORE lets kids who are crazy about sports use their enthusiasm for giving back to others." With his mitzvah project, Zach gave kids double the incentive to score!

Ryan G.—Creating Future Tennis Champions

Game: Ryan's favorite place to be is on the tennis court. Win or lose, playing tennis gives him exercise, focus, discipline, and great friendships. To share his love of the game with others, Ryan wanted to give disadvantaged kids the chance to try out his favorite sport.

Match: Through research on the Internet, Ryan and his mom located the Washington Tennis and Education Foundation (www.wtef.org) in nearby Washington, D.C. The organization provides tennis instruction and after-school enrichment through teaching academic and life skills to help kids be more successful. Ryan wrote a letter to his friends and family telling them about the amazing work of the foundation. He included his letter with his Bar

Mitzvah invitations. Ryan asked his guests to bring gently used or new rackets, warm-up suits, visors, and tennis balls to his synagogue on the day of his Bar Mitzvah. He placed large containers in the lobby to collect the tennis clothing and equipment. A few days later, Ryan and his dad brought all the donations to the tennis foundation. Ryan hopes his donations will help create more tennis enthusiasts like him.

Pierce U.—A Big-League Difference for Little League

The first inning: Pierce has played baseball since he was six. When he came up with the idea of donating used or new baseball equipment to underfunded Little League teams for his mitzvah project, his parents told him to "step up to the plate!" Pierce named his project **B**ats **A**nd **B**alls for **E**veryone, or B.A.B.E. To kick off the project, Pierce needed bins to store donated equipment. His family went to a garlic factory, which contributed three bins. Pierce washed the smelly bins out really well, attached a flyer describing his project on each, and placed the bins at local baseball fields. The next requirement was storage space for the equipment as the bins filled up. Pierce and his dad approached several storage companies, asking for donated space. After several rejections, one owner who really liked the project offered free storage for six months.

A home run: Pierce's "Campbell Little League" teammates were supportive. Due to the generosity of family, friends, and neighbors, he collected over 160 helmets and many dozens of bats, balls, gloves, baseballs, and more. Pierce enjoyed helping others and also gaining business experience: "What excited me was running this project myself. It was like having my own company. With guidance from my parents, I designed flyers, attended meetings to present my project, and wrote a press release for our local paper."

Sports Journal

Use your athletic energy to fuel positive change in the world.

What inspired you in this chapter? Jot down ideas you want to remember for possible mitzvah projects ... and beyond.

_____

_____

_____

_____

_____

_____

_____

_____

_____

_____

_____

_____

_____

_____

_____

_____

_____

_____

_____

Your World, Our World

Environment

"There are two ways to live your life. One is as
though nothing is a miracle. The other is as
though everything is a miracle."

—ALBERT EINSTEIN (1879–1955), SCIENTIST, PHILOSOPHER

Host an Earth-Friendly Bar/Bat Mitzvah Party

Go green, and not with envy, for your Bar/Bat Mitzvah. Consider sending electronic invitations instead of mailing paper ones. Use cloth instead of paper napkins. Request that your caterer serve as much locally grown food as possible. Create centerpieces that can be replanted, such as herbs, or donated, such as books. And pick party favors like saplings or seed packets that make the world more beautiful.

✔ Get It Going

Let's face it, it wouldn't be a Jewish event if you didn't have lots of food at your celebration. Make plans to donate the leftovers to a community organization, like a food bank. If your caterer is concerned she/he will be liable if anyone gets sick from the donated food, tell her/him not to worry. The federal Bill Emerson Good Samaritan Food Donation Act states: "A person or gleaner shall not be subject to civil or criminal liability arising from the nature, age, packaging or condition of apparently wholesome food or an apparently fit grocery product that the person or gleaner donates in good faith to a nonprofit organization for ultimate distribution to needy individuals."

Sew Bags to Save Bags

Even with all the promotion about going green, people are still going shopping for food, clothing, and miscellaneous purchases without bringing a reusable shopping bag. What happens to these paper and plastic bags that stores provide? Some clog drains, some kill wildlife, and some add to landfills. You can help stop the waste and destruction. Design and sew reusable cloth shopping bags to distribute to people who typically get new bags each time they shop.

✓ Get It Going

Think creatively about whom you could give your bags to. How about donating them to a food pantry so when people come for groceries, their food is packaged in a reusable bag that they are instructed to bring back when they return. Or perhaps visit a senior center in your town and give the bags to the elders there. You could even give a bag to each family who attends your Bar/Bat Mitzvah with a note explaining the benefit of reusing cloth bags versus getting plastic ones from the store.

Plant a Tree, or Two, or Three...

It's impossible to underestimate the benefits of trees. They cleanse the air, offer shade, provide homes to animals, prevent flooding, and bear fruit and nuts. You can raise money to have trees planted in Israel, in your hometown, or anywhere. Pick one of many organizations to support, such as the Jewish National Fund (www.jnf.org), an organization that plants trees in Israel; the Fruit Tree Planting Foundation (www.ftpf.org), dedicated to planting fruit trees to benefit needy populations; or the Arbor Day Foundation (www.arborday.org), with tree-planting programs in states across the United States.

✔ Get It Going

Are you planning on giving a party favor to your friends who come to your Bar/Bat Mitzvah? Why not have several trees planted in Israel in honor of your friends. A tree costs $18, and the Jewish National Fund offers over a dozen different styles of certificates from which to choose.

Grow a Garden of Healthy Delights

Imagine your delight as you tend to a vegetable garden and grow fresh food to donate to a food pantry or shelter. Then imagine the delight of the people who are able to eat your locally grown produce. Gardening for others is a great summer avocation or, if you live in a warm-weather climate, a wonderful spring, fall, or winter activity as well. Here's to your green thumb!

✔ Get It Going

Cherry tomatoes, radishes, zucchini, beets, carrots, spinach, Swiss chard, peas, peppers, lettuce, onion, leeks, and dwarf beans are all purported to be simple to grow. Before you start planting, consider your climate, available space, and the amount of time you have to devote to gardening. Also be sure to speak to the food pantry or shelter to determine which vegetables they would like most.

Be a Water Watchdog

Have you ever thought about what happens to old motor oil, paint, garden fertilizer, and swimming pool chemicals? Too often they end up washed or poured down drains. Without realizing it, people's household chemicals are flowing into creeks, rivers, and finally the ocean, polluting the water and hurting wildlife. Since many people are unaware of the links between household chemicals and water pollution, education is key. Getting the word out is where you come in!

✓ Get It Going

There are many ways you can get the word out. Start by speaking to officials at your town's Department of Public Works and Conservation Committee. Learn what they are doing and how you can help. Write an article for your school newspaper. Speak to the Parent-Teacher Organization and ask if you can include information in their e-newsletter, too. If your town holds special days for recycling paint and for dropping off hazardous household products, time your articles to promote these days.

Collect Recyclables from Others

Small recyclable batteries, ink-jet printer cartridges, bottles, cans— despite good intentions, sometimes it is hard or even impossible for people to coordinate recycling these items. For elders, transportation could be an issue. For busy professionals, time could be the problem. That's where you come to the rescue. Offer free recycling pick-up services. Specify the items, days, and times you will be collecting. Place a flyer in people's mailboxes to announce your service. Provide a way for people to contact you to sign up and to ask questions.

✓ Get It Going

Think about the best audience for your services. Is there senior housing in your town? Do you have specific neighbors who might need help? Since you will likely need a parent to transport you to the dump and recycling center, be sure to talk to your mom or dad before you make any commitments. And if you earn any money from recycling, donate the money to a green cause.

Real Kids, Real Mitzvot

Jake W.—Reuse & Recycle

Time for a turnaround: When Jake's mother delivered donations of clothing and small household items to a Hadassah thrift store, she found a sixty-year-old store in a state of disrepair. That's when Jake came up with the idea to remodel the shop. Jake assembled a team of friends and grown-ups with the right skills to give the store a long-overdue face-lift.

Lots of elbow grease: The boys cleaned the store top to bottom and gave it a fresh coat of paint. With the help of a couple of adults, they repaired shelving and added lights. They even found a few upholstered chairs to donate to make the store more comfortable. Thanks to Jake and his team, the Hadassah thrift shop is now more inviting for shoppers and employees, too.

Andy R.—Neighborhood Recycling Captain

Respect for the fields: Andy's mitzvah project was inspired by his Torah portion, which talks about respect for the environment: "Six years you may sow your field and six years you may prune your vineyard and gather in the yield. But in the seventh year the land shall have a Sabbath of complete rest" (Leviticus 25:3–4). Andy decided to show respect for the environment in a modern way, since his suburban yard has no vegetables or vines growing on it! He contacted his county's solid-waste recycling center and asked for suggestions on how he could help.

Respect for the environment: Andy learned the extent to which recycling benefits the environment. He educated neighbors about ways to support the county programs for glass, plastic, and paper recycling. He also passed out brochures to make county residents aware of the negative impact of fertilizer on water quality. Andy became so committed to environmental efforts that two years later, he is still participating in Earth Day events and town initiatives that promote recycling of technology items and safe paper shredding.

Zachary R.—Giving Used Sneakers a Second Life

Being kind to the Earth: Zach believes everyone can do more to be a friend to the Earth. At home, he constantly reminds his family to separate out all the cans, glass, and bottles for the recycling program in their town. He also saves unwanted food for a compost heap in the backyard. Zach's mom is a teacher at a school that supports a sneaker-recycling program. When he learned about this effort, Zach thought it would be a great mitzvah project.

Rescue refuse! While most people throw their stinky sneakers out in the trash, Zach decided to let people know about a way to recycle them, and he collected worn pairs for Nike's "Reuse-a-Shoe" program (www.nikereuseashoe.com). Nike recycles the entire shoe: the rubber goes into the surface of running tracks; the fabric becomes the padding for basketball courts; and the inner foam sole morphs into tough, springy tennis courts. Zach placed collection bins at his synagogue and school. He decorated them with flyers explaining his project. He also announced his project on the loudspeaker at his middle school three times a week. Zach saved almost 150 pairs of sneakers from the trash heap and delivered them to a collection center near his home. He recommends this project: "Recycling is a great mitzvah project. By reusing materials that are already harvested, we can slow down the depletion of our Earth's resources."

Environment Journal

Mother Nature will thank you when you pick a mitzvah project
that makes the world a greener place.

What inspired you in this chapter? Jot down ideas you want to
remember for possible mitzvah projects ... and beyond.

_____

_____

_____

_____

_____

_____

_____

_____

_____

_____

_____

_____

_____

_____

_____

_____

_____

_____

_____

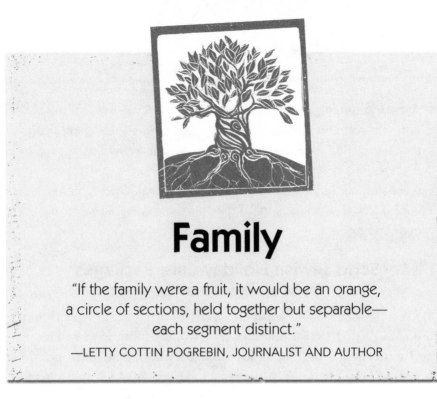

Family

"If the family were a fruit, it would be an orange,
a circle of sections, held together but separable—
each segment distinct."

—LETTY COTTIN POGREBIN, JOURNALIST AND AUTHOR

Capture Your Family's History
for Generations to Come

How many generations ago did your family come to North America? What countries did your ancestors emigrate from? Can you name your relatives in and beyond your grandparents' generation? For your mitzvah project, create your genealogy or family history to share with all your relatives. To get started, interview your parents, aunts, uncles, grandparents, great-aunts, and great-uncles. Ask them for names of relatives and where they lived so you can start to map your family tree. Then, it's time to consult historical records, including census, military, immigration, ship passenger, naturalization, and land records to find out more about your ancestors and events that occurred in their lives.

✓ Get It Going

Genealogical research is a complex process, so perhaps you could use some of the money you receive for your Bar or Bat Mitzvah to hire a professional genealogist to assist you. According to Ancestry.com, hourly rates vary from $20 to $100. Have a parent help you find a professional by consulting a local chapter of the Association for Professional Genealogists (www.apgen.org). You can also find resources on the website for the Jewish Genealogical Association (www.jewishgen.org). Once you have your family tree, make sure to give a copy to all your relatives near and far.

Send Jewish Holiday Care Packages to Your Relatives at College

Do you have cousins or brothers or sisters living at college? If they are away during Jewish holidays, it's a wonderful time to reach out and send them a little extra love and attention. Your packages do not need to be elaborate, just a personal note and a few items make it clear you are thinking of them. Everyone loves getting a package!

✔ Get It Going

Need a few ideas for what to send along? At Rosh Hashanah, pack up a small plastic bottle of honey and a loaf of homemade apple bread; for Hanukkah, send a dreidel and chocolate coins; for Tu B'Shevat, the festival of trees, mail useful recycled paper items, such as a notepad or a pocket-sized package of tissues; at Purim, share some candies and hamantaschen; and for Passover, how about a box of jellied candies or chocolate-covered matzah?

Create a Birthday Bookmark

It's tough enough to remember all the daily stuff like your homework, team practice times, and Hebrew assignments ... not to mention family members' birthdays. Here's a way for you to keep track of their special days and help relatives do so, too. Craft a birthday bookmark with the birth dates of your mom, dad, sisters, brothers, aunts, uncles, grandparents, and cousins. Organize the bookmark by month, then list the birth date and name of everyone in your extended family. Send a birthday bookmark to each person on your list, and make a separate bookmark for each side of your family.

It's an especially great way to keep your family in touch even if you're miles apart.

✓ Get It Going

Take it one step further to ensure that all family members remember each others' birthdays. A week before each family member's birthday, send an e-mail out to everyone on your list to remind each one to send greetings. Make yourself a list of dates you'll need to send reminder e-mails out, and keep it by your computer so you don't let any birthdays slip by.

Organize a Family Yard Sale for Charity

It is likely that you and your relatives have items in your homes that you don't use or need anymore. So why not sell them and donate the proceeds to a good cause? Ask your immediate family as well as grandparents, aunts, uncles, and cousins who live nearby if they have any items for a yard sale to raise money for charity. Suggest that they look around for extra sets of dishes, glasses, pots, and pans tucked away in the back of cabinets; bicycles and scooters in the garage that are no longer used; outgrown clothes; *chatchkies* (knickknacks) that are just collecting dust; baby gear … you get the idea, just about anything that could have value to someone else. In addition to supporting a good cause, family members will likely be grateful to you for motivating them to clean out space in their homes, too! If your family has a favorite charity, that's a good place to donate the money you earn. If not, solicit ideas from family members and let everyone who contributed items to the yard sale vote for a charity. Then, let majority rule.

✓ Get It Going

Once you pick a weekend day when your parents and any other willing relatives can assist you, send notification of your yard sale to your local newspaper for their print and online versions. Put posters up in high-traffic areas in your neighborhood and on bulletin boards at the local supermarket, drugstore, bakery … Send out an e-mail notification to everyone you can think of. If members of your family have a Facebook page, ask them to post a message there, too. Once you collect all the items, tag them with prices. And make sure to have plenty of change on hand the day of the sale.

Invent Sibling's Day

There's an official Mother's Day and Father's Day, so why not celebrate "Sibling's Day" to show your brother(s) and/or sister(s) how much they mean to you. Pick a weekend or holiday so school doesn't interfere. Find ways to announce the surprise day right when they wake up. How about a funny message in shaving cream on the bathroom vanity mirror? Or a homemade card waiting on the kitchen table at breakfast? Then make sure to fill the day with activities, foods, and messages that will make your sibling(s) smile.

✔ Get It Going

Start by making a list of your siblings' favorite foods, music, hobbies, and more. Ask your parents to help you prepare your siblings' preferred sweet treat, sandwich, and dinner meal. Put together a playlist of their favorite tunes. Play their favorite games with them, even if that means the ninety-ninth game of Bananagrams or Boggle in a week! Help them clean their room or do their chores for them. And end the day with a funny poem or note about what they mean to you.

Create a Family Facebook Group

Decades ago, Jewish families stayed in the neighborhoods where they were raised and often held cousins' clubs on Sunday afternoons at *bubbe*'s house. Mingling with different generations was how families shared laughs and wisdom. Today, our families are typically spread across different time zones, let alone different towns. By creating a family Facebook page, your family can stay in closer touch.

✓ Get It Going

Ask your parents' permission to organize your family Facebook effort. Unless your parents are tech-savvy, they probably can't help you create the page, but they can help you in other ways. They can give you contact information for distant relatives, offer you some entertaining family stories to post, and dig out favorite photos of Great-Uncle Mort's Bar Mitzvah, Cousin Dara's baby pictures, and Nana's wedding.

Real Kids, Real Mitzvot

Daniel M.—Honoring Grandpa's Courage

Insight: Daniel's grandfather has been blind since the age of eleven, when he had spinal meningitis. As an adult, Daniel's grandfather moved his family from a rural to an urban neighborhood to attend law school outside of Boston. That's when he participated in an intensive "Seeing Eye dog" training program (www.seeingeye.org) so he could safely and independently navigate in a city.

Eyesight: For his mitzvah project, Daniel asked family and friends to pledge money to the Israel Guide Dog Center for the Blind (www.israelguide.org) so that visually impaired Israelis could benefit from the assistance of a guide dog, just as his grandfather still does today. Daniel tied his love of baseball to his fund-raising efforts. He asked friends and family to pledge a specific amount for every strikeout he pitched in Little League. Luckily for Daniel, and for the Israel Guide Dog Center, Daniel had a great season and raised over $10,000.

Rachel K.—Carrying on Grandma's Mitzvah

Following grandma's stitches: Rachel decided to honor the memory of her grandmother when she chose her Bat Mitzvah project. Over the years, her grandma had donated handmade pillows to a local school for children with autism. Rachel made a pledge to do the same.

Pillows at the party: At Rachel's Bat Mitzvah celebration, her friends—nearly forty girls and boys—created colorful pillows while the parents enjoyed hors d'oeuvres and cocktails. Before the party, Rachel and her mom bought hand towels with animals printed on the front. Rachel's mom poked holes through the sides of the cloths with a knitting needle. Then, both of them precut dozens of strips of brightly hued yarn. At the party's start, the teens had fun stitching up each side of the towels and stuffing them to make pillows. Rachel delivered the pillows to the same school that her grandmother had helped. The school gave the children some of the pillows to take home and saved the others for the students to use at school during naptime.

Jesse G.—For His Cousin and His Fellow Servicemen and Servicewomen

Operation Salami Drop: Jesse's family has been active in the U.S. Air Force. In fact, he had a cousin stationed in Afghanistan. Deployment of troops, bombs, gunfire, and warfare is not something Jesse can ignore on the television news. Because Jesse and his family know very well how it feels to have a loved one at risk in a war zone, he wanted to do something for the U.S. troops in the Middle East. Jesse decided to support a program at a deli near his home. The deli will send a salami to any U.S. soldier for $10. Jesse set a goal for himself—to raise $3,650. That amount would be enough to send a salami to a different soldier every day for an entire year!

For the troops: Jesse got up his gumption and starting speaking to groups about his goal to raise the $3,650. He talked at Veterans Clubs, the Kiwanis Club, at a table he set up outside his local grocery store, and at a town-wide photo session for the recreational soccer teams. Each time, he described his goal and asked for donations. The local paper also wrote a story about his project. Through all his hard work, Jesse collected almost twice as much money as he had set out to fund-raise. What's more, each month for a year, Jesse helped out at the deli, packing up the salamis for their trip to the war zone. Jesse included a letter about his project in every package. "Doing a mitzvah project inspired me to support our troops and help 'Operation Salami Drop!'" Jesse explained.

Caroline D., Caroline G., Laura G., Molly B., and Sara G.—
Preparing Dinner for Families with Children in the Hospital

Comfort food: Five girls who attend the same temple joined together to make meals for families of children undergoing medical treatments at Boston hospitals. These families were staying at the Ronald McDonald House (www.rmhc.org), a "home-away-from-home," to be close by their hospitalized children at little or no cost.

A home-cooked meal: Each girl and her mother took a turn planning the dinner, shopping for the ingredients, and hosting the other girls at their house to cook the meal. After Sunday school, the girls prepared family-tested recipes for chicken, lasagna, rice, salad, cookies, cupcakes, and other favorite foods. Once the cooking and cleanup were complete, the host mom and her daughter dropped the food off at the Ronald McDonald House. While the girls learned to cook together, more importantly, they learned how good it feels to spend Sunday afternoons helping others.

Jamie T.—A Service in Poland

Honoring the past: Jamie connected her mitzvah project to her Bat Mitzvah service. She and her family decided to honor the memory of family members by holding her Bat Mitzvah service in Krakow, Poland. Many of Jamie's relatives perished during the Nazi occupation of Poland, and several others, including her grandfather, had escaped. In fact, her grandfather was on the last train out of Poland on his way back to school in England at the time of the invasion, and Jamie's great-grandmother survived the war on "Schindler's list." Surrounded by twenty-five members of her family, including her uncle who is a rabbi, Jamie was the first Bat Mitzvah ever in the Krakow synagogue.

Honoring the future: Jamie decided to help the Jewish Community Center in Krakow (www.jcckrakow.org), which fosters Jewish awareness through Shabbat services and community events. She set out to collect 995,000 pennies to represent that number of Polish Jewish children who died in the Holocaust. Through flyers, talking to classes at her synagogue, e-mails, and discussions with friends, Jamie raised nearly 250,000 pennies. "I was so excited to give the donation myself to the JCC in Poland. There aren't many Jewish families there, and they really need our support," Jamie confided.

Sam B.—Paying Tribute to His Birthplace and His Dad

Honoring Colombia: While Sam participated in a group mitzvah project through his religious school, he also wanted to perform a mitzvah that was uniquely personal. Sam was born in Colombia. His memory of his birthplace was shaped by photos and stories of his trip back to Colombia with his parents to adopt his little sister when he was only three years old. Sam knew he wanted to do something related to Colombia, but what? One idea that Sam, a soccer enthusiast, had was to raise money to buy soccer equipment for the Casa de Maria orphanage he and his sister lived at after birth. Sam's mom spoke to the orphanage director about the idea. The director informed his mom about the pressing need to raise funds to build a new wing so that the orphanage could help more children. Sam was up for that challenge!

Honoring his dad's memory: For several years, Sam had participated in the American Cancer Society's Relay for Life (www.relayforlife.org). Sam lost his dad to cancer when he was only five years old, and each year he worked hard to get sponsors and raise money for cancer research. This year, he asked people to donate to Casa de Maria's building fund instead. Sam sent a letter to everyone he could think of—friends, neighbors, relatives. His letter from the heart generated several thousand dollars in donations. Sam's mom and the lawyers who had helped with his and his sister's adoptions also contributed. Together, Sam, his mom, his younger sister, and his stepdad flew to Colombia to present Casa de Maria with the check. They were welcomed by many of the staff his mother remembered from years before. And due to Sam's hard work, the new wing of the orphanage was named after Sam's dad.

Family Journal

The whole *mishpachah* will be proud of you whether you help one relative or many.

What inspired you in this chapter? Jot down ideas you want to remember for possible mitzvah projects ... and beyond.

_____

_____

_____

_____

_____

_____

_____

_____

_____

_____

_____

_____

_____

_____

_____

_____

_____

_____

_____

_____

Friends, Neighbors & Your Community

"Behold, how good and how pleasant it is for brethren
to dwell together in unity!"

—*HINEI MAH TOV* LYRICS (PSALM 133:1)

Organize an Anti-bullying Essay Contest

Bullying is a problem in many middle schools, likely including your own. Some kids use physical intimidation to bully. Other kids play mind games, insulting or excluding a kid to torment him or her. Whether you have witnessed or been the target of bullying, everyone benefits when kids speak out in outrage. There are many ways you can help. Tell a caring adult about a bullying situation. You can also support a kid who is being bullied by walking home with him or her after school, by sitting together at lunch or on the school bus, or by choosing him or her for your team in gym. If you feel you can do so safely, you could also tell the bully to cut it out. One way to make anti-bullying the focus of your mitzvah project is to sponsor an essay contest to raise awareness of the issue and inspire classmates to take a stand against kids harassing other kids.

✓ Get It Going

Find a teacher at your school who will work with you on an anti-bullying essay contest. You will need to solicit a few adults to read the essays and pick the winners—perhaps your principal, your gym teacher, a youth police officer, and a couple of clergy in town could join in with a classroom teacher. Ask a local ice-cream store to donate free sundaes for the essay contest winner and runner-up and a friend each. Maybe the shop will also donate an ice-cream cake to the winner's class! Or you could buy the sundae gift certificates with your own money as part of your mitzvah project.

Offer Hours of Free Babysitting

Mothers and fathers of young children often have little free time. Some have additional demands such as caring for an elderly relative, looking for a new job, or helping a friend who is not well. Virtually all moms and dads would appreciate an hour or two to shop without children in tow, take a run or a walk, meet a friend for coffee, or sit and read a good book. Create babysitting vouchers to give as gifts to mothers or fathers whose body and spirit could use a little recharging. Include after-school or weekend dates and times that are good for you to offer your services.

✓ Get It Going

Does your temple have a Caring Committee or group that helps members going through a stressful time? If so, they could be a great source of names of moms and dads who could use some free babysitting or parent helper hours. Ask your parents for suggestions as well. If you have younger siblings, be sure to give your parents a voucher, too!

Support Soldiers from Your Area

Can you imagine how difficult it must be for soldiers to head away from home? Whether they are leaving for an overseas assignment or to a base somewhere in North America, undoubtedly it is a very emotional time for them. Since gestures of gratitude will certainly be appreciated, go to the airport (or organize a group of friends to join you) to provide a warm send-off and welcome home to the men and women who sacrifice so much to strengthen and protect our country. To learn when groups of soldiers will be leaving or returning, contact your local military base.

✓ Get It Going

What can you bring to the airport to show your appreciation? Make big, bright signs that say "Thank you," "Safe travels," or "Welcome home." You could even assemble small care packages for soldiers shipping out. Packs of chewing gum, mints, pre-paid phone cards, books, magazines, playing cards, lip balm, and handwritten notes are just a few of the items you can include.

Deliver Purim Packages

In the *Megillah*, the book of Esther, we are told that Purim should be a holiday in recognition of how the Jews of ancient Persia were saved from annihilation. Mordechai, Esther's cousin, also urged that gift giving to the needy should be part of the Purim remembrance. So put down your *groggers* for a bit and be part of this Purim caring tradition by making *mishloach manot*, or food baskets. You can share these baskets of treats with friends who are in need of good cheer, whether they are Jewish or not.

✓ Get It Going

If you're not sure who to make baskets for, contact your local Jewish Family Services agency or your rabbi to identify people who might enjoy a Purim surprise. Decorate shopping bags, boxes, or baskets to hold food items, such as dried fruits, candy, energy bars, crackers, and nuts. And wouldn't it be extra special to bake hamantaschen (traditional triangle pastries) to include in your Purim present?

Be a Study Buddy

Does one particular subject come easily to you? What's the square root of 121? Maybe solving math problems is second nature to you. *Parlez-vous français?* Perhaps speaking a foreign language is fun for you. Are you a whiz at reading Hebrew? Whatever your best subject is, why not offer to help a student who could use a little extra help in that area? Suggest a day and time you are able to get together once a week, maybe after school or on the weekend, to review homework, study for tests, and share your learning tricks and techniques.

✓ Get It Going

To find another kid who could use a little extra help, contact the guidance counselor or special education director at your school, or a contact person at your synagogue. Explain your study buddy idea, and ask the grown-up to reach out to prospective study buddies on your behalf. Once they find a good match and make an introduction for you, get ready to step in and make studying a little more productive and fun.

Host a Charity Softball Game for Friends and Neighbors

A great way to raise money for a cause and build community at the same time is to host a softball game in honor or memory of someone special to you—it could be a relative who has beat cancer, a grandparent who has passed away from a heart attack, or a friend living with diabetes. Invite friends and family to join in a fun game of softball for a small donation. Ask people to sign up in advance to make sure you field two balanced teams with a range of players of different ages and athletic abilities. Speak to the recreation department coordinator of your town to reserve a nearby baseball field. Bring water and snacks, bats, balls, bases, and gloves. And select someone special for the honor of throwing out the first pitch!

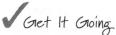

✓ Get It Going

However you promote your softball game for charity—online, e-mail, flyers—be sure to provide a profile of the person you are honoring or remembering, as well as a description of the charity to which you will donate the funds. This will surely draw more people to participate not only to have fun, but also to support a worthy cause.

Real Kids, Real Mitzvot

Sam M.—Forging a Friendship over Lunch

The power of a bond: After Sam read about the organization Best Buddies International (www.bestbuddies.org), which fosters one-to-one friendships between people with and without intellectual disabilities, he wanted to create a bond with a special needs student at his own middle school.

Strengthened over time: Sam spoke to one of the special needs teachers, and together they came up with a plan. Once a week for Sam's entire seventh-grade year, he sat with his buddy, a boy with Down's syndrome, at lunch in the school cafeteria. At first, Sam found it difficult to relate and know what to talk about. Soon the boys found common interests, like food, school, and sports. And sometimes one of Sam's friends would join them, too. In the end, it didn't take long for the two boys to become friends and look forward to their lunch together.

Molly C.—Speaking Up against Anti-Semitism

Hurt can lead to healing: Molly and both her siblings have felt the sting of anti-Semitism at their school, where there are few Jewish kids. Once, a boy threw pennies at her younger brother on the school bus, taunting him, "Hey, Jew-boy, aren't you going to pick those pennies up?" And Molly experienced anti-Semitism when a classmate of hers continued to draw swastikas (the symbol of the Nazi regime) even after Molly explained how much the symbols upset her. Molly hesitantly spoke up about this incident to her teacher and principal. They spoke to the girl about why her behavior was unacceptable. A couple of years later in social studies class, Molly was assigned the seat next to that same girl, coincidentally just when the class was about to study the Holocaust. Molly felt uncomfortable and wanted to move her seat, although she never did. But when the unit on the Holocaust was completed, the girl handed Molly a long letter apologizing for drawing swastikas and for the pain she had caused. This letter prompted Molly to learn even more about the Holocaust. She visited the Holocaust, Genocide & Human Rights Education Center (www.hghrec.org) in Lincroft, New Jersey. Through that center she met Mrs. Helena Flaum, a survivor, who shared her perspective: "Molly, we can forgive, but we must never forget. You taught that girl something valuable when you spoke up."

Education can heal, too: Molly shared these experiences in her Bat Mitzvah speech and pointed out how befriending Mrs. Flaum changed her. Unfortunately, another anti-Semitic episode happened to Molly in school just a couple of weeks after her Bat Mitzvah. Reluctantly again, Molly bravely took action. With her principal's help, she organized a Tolerance Club and brought a group of survivors to talk to the entire eighth grade. Molly believes, "If we can educate one person at a time, and they in turn educate one person, we just may get closer to conquering ignorance and hatred in our world."

Elliot S.—The Mitzvah Meter Man

Running late: Elliot knows firsthand how frustrating it is for drivers to get parking tickets because their meter runs out. No, Elliot does not drive, but he is often with his mom when she returns to her car only to find her meter expired and a ticket on her windshield.

Twenty-five cents is all it takes: Elliot's mom's despair inspired his mitzvah project. Elliot walked around the downtown of his small hometown looking for expired parking meters. Each time he found one, he inserted a quarter and left a note, "You have been saved by the Mitzvah Meter Man. Please pay it forward." It made Elliot happy to imagine the smiles he brought to all the people he saved from receiving tickets.

Lindsay H.—A Time for Tutoring

3 times 8: Lindsay always loved math and younger kids, so she was delighted to find out about a program called Math Adventures and Word Play, a program in Teaneck, New Jersey, that provides children with free tutoring. Once a week for about two hours, Lindsay volunteered to tutor math at a church in a nearby town. Every Saturday, she helped one of the second- through sixth-graders prepare homework or study for a test.

Feeling great: Many of the kids attending the program were not able to afford tutors. Lindsay explained, "It felt great to know I was able to use my talent to help others who struggled. The most rewarding part of my tutoring was when a child understood something for the first time. I felt great knowing I helped them pass their next test, even if it was just understanding how to multiply 3 by 2." Lindsay enjoyed tutoring so much that she is in her fourth year.

Little did she know that what began as a simple mitzvah project would turn into something she looks forward to doing every week!

Haley A.—Hosting Happy Birthdays

Spreading joy: Haley knew her thirteenth birthday was sure to be a happy day, since her Bat Mitzvah was on her actual birthday. She took this coincidence as an omen to dedicate her mitzvah project to making other kids' birthdays happy, too. Through Birthday Wishes (www.birthdaywishes.org), an organization that serves homeless children, Haley hosted a party for two-year-old Isaiah at the shelter where he and his mom were living.

Sharing gifts: After Isaiah's guests were done eating cake, playing beanbag toss, decorating visors, and getting temporary tattoos, they waited their turn to play with the new toy car Isaiah got from Haley for his birthday. Impressed by the little boy's patience, Haley and her mom ordered more cars after the party and sent one to each of Isaiah's friends at the shelter. But that's not all the birthday cheer Haley spread; she also created themed "birthday in a bag" centerpieces of cake mixes, frosting, paper goods, and party favors for the tables at her *Kiddush* luncheon and donated the bags to Birthday Wishes after her Bat Mitzvah.

Abby H.—Helping Homeless Children

Reaching out: Abby loves children, so finding a way to support kids in need was her goal. Through friends, Abby's mother learned of Cradles to Crayons (C2C, www.boston.cradlestocrayons.org), an organization that provides homeless and other children in need with essentials to be safe, warm, valued, and ready to learn.

Chipping in: Abby and her mom went to the C2C donation center to sort clothing, toys, books, school supplies, and other items into bags for needy families. Abby also asked her Bat Mitzvah guests to bring school supplies to her synagogue to donate to C2C. Abby must have been very persuasive. The donated supplies filled a large truck!

Sophie D.-R.—Collecting School Supplies

Home: Sophie found inspiration for her mitzvah project in her Torah portion, *Lech Lecha* (Genesis 12:1–17:27), about Abraham and Sarah having to leave their home and go to an unknown place. Sophie thought a lot about how much having a home meant to her and her family. She wanted to help kids in her own community who had no home of their own. Sophie's mom suggested she focus on the First Place School (www.firstplaceschool.org), which offers free housing, education, and support services to families facing homelessness in Seattle. Sophie made up her mind to collect back-to-school items so kids could start off the school year with fresh school supplies.

School: Sophie put collection bins at her synagogue, at her school, and outside her house. She also included information about her project with her Bat Mitzvah invitations. She collected more than fourteen big bags of backpacks, pens, paper, crayons, glue sticks, scissors, and more. The bags filled an entire car! After delivering the supplies, Sophie wanted to do more: "I was glad that I could help the kids get excited for school. I hope when I'm older that I can volunteer in person at the First Place School."

Garrett L.—Care Packages for the Troops

Starting with sweets: During the fall of sixth grade, Garrett was trying to decide on an idea for his mitzvah project. The war in Iraq was very much in the news at that time. At his school, Garrett's teacher organized a Halloween candy drive to create care packages for American soldiers overseas. Garrett asked her how he could get involved in the effort.

Continuing with care: Garrett volunteered with Operation Buckeye (www.operationbuckeye.org), an organization in Ohio that sends care packages of food, toiletries, and entertainment items to the troops in Iraq and Afghanistan. Continuing his support after his Bar Mitzvah, Garrett has organized fund-raisers, packed care packages, and written grant letters soliciting donations. One Veterans Day, he organized a raffle at a Minor League baseball game and raised $1,400 for Operation Buckeye. Garrett has received many thank-you letters back from soldiers. Sometimes the troops even include photos of their group or patches from their uniforms.

Kate L., Jesse L., Ryan M., Jordan S., and Joey M.— Fund-raising for the Local Community

A group challenge: Jewish Aid in Australia (JAA, www.jewishaid.org.au) is an organization dedicated to mobilizing the Australian Jewish community to participate in humanitarian projects locally and overseas. JAA put out "The $10 Challenge," to a B'nai Mitzvah class to motivate kids to find imaginative ways to make a small amount of seed money grow and grow to help those in need. Kate, Jesse, Ryan, Jordan, and Joey took on this "pay it forward" challenge.

Sweets for change: The kids formed small groups to put their entrepreneurial skills to the test. Their idea—to host a lolly (lollipop) drive at their schools—was a huge success. The kids turned their initial $30 investment into $450! With their proceeds, they purchased a sporting goods gift certificate to help establish a sports club for the local Sudanese community. The kids presented their gift to the Sudanese community at a special barbecue held at a neighborhood park the day after Yom Kippur. "People at my school were asking me why I was so keen to participate in the challenge. My answer was always the same—to help someone less fortunate than I am. When we gave the money to the Sudanese community, it felt like I had just done the greatest mitzvah, to put other people before myself," reported Jordan.

Amy Z.—Righting a Wrong in the Community

Hearing bad news: The year before her Bat Mitzvah, Amy saw an Atlanta news broadcast and learned that a local shelter had been robbed. All the gifts they had collected for their clients were stolen days before their holiday party. Amy was devastated—how could anyone steal from people who have so little? That year, she used the money saved in her piggy bank to replace as many gifts as she could afford and delivered them to the shelter. She was determined to bring happiness to as many as she could.

Making good news: After her Bat Mitzvah, Amy used $400 of her gifts to throw her own holiday party for children living in a homeless shelter. With the help of her parents, she reached out to Jewish Family & Career Services of Atlanta (www.yourtoolsforliving.org) and organized a holiday party for twenty-five kids at a local shelter. She invited her friends to join her, and together they hosted the first "Amy's Holiday Party." Amy did not realize at the time that a community celebration of this kind did not exist in the Atlanta area. Sixteen years later, Amy's Holiday Party is now hosted by a nonprofit organization called Creating Connected Communities (CCC), which Amy founded in 2010. The event now hosts close to six hundred children and their families from over

thirty homeless shelters, foster-care systems, and refugee centers around Atlanta. More than three hundred teens volunteer from all over the city, and local businesses, foundations,
individuals, and many Jewish agencies lend their support to
make Amy's Holiday Party a community-wide success.

Friends, Neighbors, & Your Community Journal

Friends, whether new or old, will surely appreciate
your acts of kindness.

What inspired you in this chapter? Jot down ideas you want to
remember for possible mitzvah projects … and beyond.

_____

_____

_____

_____

_____

_____

_____

_____

_____

_____

_____

_____

_____

_____

_____

_____

_____

_____

_____

_____

_____

Global Community

"I have always believed that the majority of the people want peace and are ready to take risks for peace."
—YITZHAK RABIN (1922–1995), FIFTH PRIME MINISTER OF ISRAEL

Teach a Man to Fish

Do you agree with the saying "Give a man a fish and you have fed him for today. Teach a man to fish and you have fed him for a lifetime"? World hunger is a terrible problem that you can help address by adhering to this saying. For example, the not-for-profit Heifer International (www.heifer.org) provides livestock and agricultural training to families in developing countries. By raising money for this organization, you enable a family in Zambia or Nepal to have its own goat to supply quarts of milk, or a family in Cameroon or the Caribbean to have chicks to supply nutritious eggs to eat and sell. There are unlimited ways to earn the money to donate. In keeping with the cooking theme, how about holding bake sales in your community?

✓ Get It Going

Where can you hold bake sales to reach a lot of hungry kids? Get permission from your synagogue to set up a table outside

147

the religious school classrooms where parents and kids pass as Sunday and weekday Hebrew school lets out. How about at the bus stop or the path by your neighborhood elementary school? Or sell your goods at the town fields where kids' soccer, base-ball, or lacrosse teams play.

Include a sign about the organization to which you'll be donating the money. It will surely encourage more people to buy your home-baked goods.

Send a Ugandan Child to School

It's virtually impossible to imagine your life and your future without school. Did you know that millions of kids are not able to go to school because in many countries schools are not free? In northern Uganda, the country with one of the longest-running wars in Africa, the educational system is in desperate condition. Communities are in ruin. Clean water, school buildings, school supplies, and technology are very limited. Most children cannot afford tuition, and schools need to be rebuilt. How can you help? A $420 donation to the Invisible Children's Legacy Fund at www.invisiblechildren.com will send a Ugandan child to school for an entire year!

✓ Get It Going

To give the precious gift of education, you could pledge a portion of the money you receive for your Bar/Bat Mitzvah to the Invisible Children's Legacy Fund and let friends and family know how many kids you hope to send to school for a year. Or you could do thirty-five odd jobs and charge $12 each—what about washing cars, walking dogs, or watering plants? You can also help send a Ugandan kid to school by purchasing books through the website betterworldbooks.com/invisiblechildren. Consider making your book purchase do double duty. Use the books in the centerpieces at your Bar/Bat Mitzvah celebration, and then donate the books to a library or school in need.

Support Ethiopian Jewish Teens in Israel

Imagine moving to a country where virtually everything is different than you are used to. That's the difficult reality for Ethiopian immigrants to Israel. Most have had no formal education and cannot read or write Amharic, the language of Ethiopia, let alone Hebrew. In addition to a new language, Ethiopian immigrants are faced with adjusting to life in a technologically advanced society, a new climate, with unfamiliar religious rituals, and a very different status for women. The Ethiopian National Project (ENP) provides educational and social opportunities for Ethiopian-Israeli teenagers. For your mitzvah project, why not raise money to help Ethiopian kids build a productive life in their new country? Visit the ENP website to learn more: http://www.enp.org.il/.

✓ Get It Going

If there is an Ethiopian restaurant near where you live, organize a fund-raising dinner at the restaurant. Talk to the restaurant manager about hosting a dinner to support ENP. Plan a menu for a set price per person. Invite your friends and their parents, and charge more than the cost of the dinner so you can raise money for ENP. In your invitation, explain why you are hosting this dinner; write about the plight of Ethiopian-Jewish teens in Israel. If you can't find an Ethiopian restaurant nearby, you could prepare an Ethiopian meal at your house and invite guests. Again, make sure to charge more than the cost of the ingredients ... and make sure at least one parent is willing to help you cook! Don't forget to include in the invitation a way for friends to make a donation even if they can't attend your restaurant or home-cooked meal.

Sponsor a Child in a Developing Country

If you are looking for a mitzvah project that starts as you prepare for your Bar/Bat Mitzvah but continues for years after, then consider sponsoring a child in a developing country. For about $30 a month, you can support a boy or girl in need. Besides helping improve another kid's life, you'll learn firsthand about the realities of growing up in a completely different environment than your own and most likely develop a friendship through correspondence. Think hard about whether you can make a multiyear commitment of time and money.

✓ Get It Going

There are many child sponsorship charities, so evaluate your options. Find out what happens to your money, and make sure the sponsored child benefits directly from the sponsorship. Can you support a child in Israel or another country that is important to you? Will you be able to communicate with the child you sponsor?

Help Refugees Resettle in Safer Places

Every Jewish person from the United States and Canada has a relative on his or her family tree who immigrated to North America for a better life. Maybe that relative was looking for a place to practice religion in peace. Maybe that relative was seeking an escape from hardship. Today, many people immigrate for similar reasons. You can help the settlement of refugees from troubled places around the globe by supporting HIAS, the Hebrew Immigrant Aid Society, started in 1881, which today provides services to Jewish as well as non-Jewish immigrants and refugees. Did you know that in 1979, HIAS helped Sergey Brin, a co-founder of Google, and his family escape anti-Semitism in the former Soviet Union and get established in Maryland? Visit www.hias.org to learn more about the many services HIAS offers to those in need, regardless of their religion, nationality, or ethnic background.

✓ Get It Going

Today, HIAS aids people in Europe, the Middle East, Africa, and Latin America. To honor HIAS, host a food court at your synagogue and serve food from countries where HIAS helps. Decorate the room with posters and the tables with flags from these countries, and donate a portion of the money you receive as gifts to the organization.

Help Get Clean Water to Those Who Need It

Clean water is something we all use every day without thinking—showering, brushing teeth, filling sports bottles.... Whenever you need it, you can turn on a faucet. But more people in the world have cell phones than have access to a flush toilet. Water sanitation problems cause more deaths each year than war does. And millions of women and girls in developing countries spend hours a day, sometimes in dangerous circumstances, in search of their family's water. These problems are preventable. You can help build wells, promote sanitation education, and more by supporting organizations that work to bring clean water to places such as Africa, India, and Central America. Check out organizations online, including www.water.org, founded by Matt Damon, and www.blueplanetnetwork.org, to help improve the lives of many around the world.

✓ Get It Going

One way you can help support pure water for the developing world is by pledging to drink only water as your beverage for two weeks. Give up soda and sports drinks for that time period, figure out how much money you saved, and donate that amount to a water charity. Don't think of your donation as just a "drop in the bucket." Every contribution counts. Challenge your family and friends to join in, too. In addition to raising money, your actions will teach everyone around you about the importance of safe and clean water.

Real Kids, Real Mitzvot

Greg and Jeff D.—Working with Their Dad in Rural Villages

Back-breaking work: One year after the other, Greg and Jeff joined their dad and his Rotary Club on a community service trip to rural villages in the Dominican Republic. For much of the time, the boys helped install two-hundred-pound bio-water filters and then surround the filters with sand and gravel.

Mind-enhancing experience: Jeff and Greg kept diaries of their service trip to capture observations and feelings:

> *"The Dominican people have very little education and most don't understand that they are drinking bacteria in the water that could make them really sick. It is amazing how the Rotary helps this community, but still the conditions of the houses are bad. They only got electricity two years ago. All the kitchens are outside. I haven't seen any real beds, and there are girls pregnant at fourteen. The people in the community never smile if they are older than school-age. We helped at a clinic today. The lady at the clinic was teaching both kids and adults how to wash their hands and how to brush their teeth properly. Later today, we were talking about how their culture is different. The children have to bike to school, and if their bike is broken, they don't go. The Rotary has given this school most of its supplies. Their life is so different from ours. We take so much for granted."*

Livia B.—Sharing a Service Trip to Peru

Learning through service: Livia was inspired by her Torah portion, *Kedoshim* (Leviticus 19:1–20:27), which gets to the heart of *tikkun olam*—treating others as you'd wish to be treated. She recognizes how fortunate she is to have had the chance to participate in a service learning trip as a pivotal part of her Bat Mitzvah experience—volunteering at a children's home in Lima, Peru, with a group called Global Volunteers (www.globalvolunteers.org) for the two weeks of her spring break.

Learning through sharing: Livia took lots and lots of photos in Peru to share with her classmates at a middle school assembly. Her goal: to educate kids about these orphans' lives and needs and to inspire her friends to find a way to help kids in need, too. Livia truly understands the incredible power of kids treating other kids as they wish to be treated.

Melissa Z.—Making the Road Less Traveled Safer

Out and about: Melissa loves to travel and wanted her mitzvah project to help children in other countries. One of Melissa's teachers had started an organization called ASIRT, the Association for Safe International Road Travel (www.asirt.org). So Melissa approached her to see if there were something she could do through ASIRT to help kids overseas.

Out of harm's way: Brainstorming together, they identified a problem in developing countries that Melissa could address. With no public transportation, many children walk from place to place on streets without sidewalks and streetlights, making it difficult for drivers to see pedestrians after dark. As you can imagine, walking in the pitch black of night in these poorer locations can be very dangerous, even fatal. Melissa used money from her Bat Mitzvah gifts to buy one thousand reflective armbands for ASIRT to distribute to children in developing countries so they can walk more safely at night.

Jenna R.—Sneakers for Rwanda

Bare feet: Jenna was trying to decide on a mitzvah project when a story in a local school paper caught her eye. A woman who traveled to Rwanda for business was asking for donations of gently used sneakers. During her trips to this African country, she saw dozens of children playing tennis in bare feet. This image spoke deeply to Jenna; she loved tennis and couldn't imagine playing without sneakers on her feet.

A great feat: Jenna spread the word to her synagogue and school communities about her sneaker collection effort and amassed nearly four hundred pairs. Jenna's mom said their house looked like a tennis warehouse after she and her parents boxed up all of the tennis-related items. It took almost a year's worth of trips for the businesswoman to transport all of the sneakers Jenna collected for the kids in Rwanda. Now hundreds of kids can run like the pros when they are dashing for the perfect shot.

Drew B.—Thinking Globally

Trouble across the seas: When the tsunami struck Indonesia in October 2010, television stations and news outlets worldwide covered the tragedy for days. But many people soon forgot the suffering of the thousands of people forced to flee their homes. Not Drew. He responded to the disaster by rounding up a few friends and brainstorming a mitzvah project. Together, they decided to sell candy and give the money to help the victims of the tsunami.

Helping hands reach out: Drew and his friends made hundreds of chocolate lollipops. They set up a table inside of a local supermarket and sold each pop for $1. They collected $375 that day and donated the money to Save the Children Federation (www.savethechildren.org), an international organization helping kids in need around the world. Drew liked working for a cause: "I appreciated the whole idea of this nonprofit project. A terrible thing happened that left people homeless and in shock. This mitzvah project let us help kids who we will never meet, but who need clothes, food, and shelter just like we do."

Global Community Journal

Reach out across the miles to help people in faraway cities, countries, or even continents.

What inspired you in this chapter? Jot down ideas you want to remember for possible mitzvah projects ... and beyond.

_____

_____

_____

_____

_____

_____

_____

_____

_____

_____

_____

_____

_____

_____

_____

_____

_____

_____

_____

_____

_____

Israel

"Our hope is not lost—
That hope of two millennia,
To be a free people in our land,
The land of Zion and Jerusalem."

—LAST LINES FROM *HATIKVAH*, ISRAELI NATIONAL ANTHEM

Support the Soldiers Who Protect Our Jewish Homeland

At the age of eighteen, almost all Israelis are drafted into the Israel Defense Forces (IDF) to defend Israel's borders and guarantee the safety of its people. Friends of the Israel Defense Forces (FIDF) is a nonprofit group dedicated to the well-being of the men and women who serve in the IDF as well as the families of fallen soldiers. The FIDF website explains, "Their job is to look after Israel. Ours is to look after them." You can help by raising money to donate to one of the FIDF programs: Education & Culture, Wellbeing & Recreation, Lone Soldiers, Bereaved Families, Medical, and Construction Projects. A donation of $110 provides two $55 gift vouchers for a soldier—one at Rosh Hashanah and one at Passover; $120 enables a soldier to enjoy a week's vacation at a rest and relaxation center, complete with athletic fields and equipment, a swimming pool, game room, theater, and computer center. Learn more at www.fidf.org.

✓ Get It Going

Read this message from a soldier to understand how appreciative Israeli soldiers are of any support you can offer:

> *"Both my parents died when I was sixteen, and since then I have been alone in this world, apart from my brothers, whom I see only when I am on leave. But since the very first day of enlisting, I have met wonderful people who take good care of me and assist me—making me feel that I have found a home. You can imagine how hard it is to be alone in the world, and to manage on your own when you are not even twenty. But thanks to the support of the Friends of the Israel Defense Forces (FIDF) and wonderful people like you—a support that included Special Aid—a washing machine and a closet—I feel so much better; I feel stronger to serve my country and contribute all I can to the IDF. Thanks to you and your families, and to FIDF, I can continue with my life as usual"*
>
> *—Corporal Y., Nachal Brigade*

Make Your Voice Heard in Support of Israel

Speaking up in support of Israel makes a big difference. When you hear about current events that affect Israel, you can write letters or e-mails to your representative and senators in Washington, D.C. For example, if you are outraged by terrorist attacks, ask your public officials to condemn the violence. If you learn about new Israeli legislation that you believe is not in the best interests of Israel or will jeopardize U.S.-Israeli relations, contact Israel's prime minister to make your voice heard. You can even go one step further and reach out to friends and relatives to get them to join you. Provide background information on the issue you want them to write about, your point of view, a sample note they can send, and contact information so it's easy for them to make their voices heard.

✓ Get It Going

How can you find out the names and contact information for members of Congress? Simply go to www.contactingthecongress.org and fill in your address. To contact the Israeli prime minister and other Israeli officials, go to www.gov.il and click on "Government Ministries," and then "Prime Minister's Office."

Throw a Peace Party

War and conflict plague the Middle East, but you can help young people move their region one step closer to understanding and peaceful coexistence. Through an organization called Seeds of Peace, Egyptian, Israeli, Jordanian, and Palestinian youth come together at a camp in Maine to develop empathy, respect, and confidence as well as leadership, communication, and negotiation skills. Support the internationally acclaimed conflict resolution work by throwing a "peace party." Invite friends and ask them to make a financial donation or to donate materials the organization needs—such as paper goods, art supplies, and sports equipment—for the party entrance fee. At the party, have the Seeds of Peace videos running and printed materials around for friends to see. Organize games and contests and give Seeds of Peace T-shirts for prizes.

✓ Get It Going

Go to www.seedsofpeace.org to read and watch videos about the organization's work and learn about the many ways you can help sow seeds of peace. If throwing a party is not for you, there are other ways to be an ambassador of peace. You could make a presentation about Seeds of Peace to your temple class (the organization offers a PowerPoint presentation on their site), introduce the social studies teachers at your school to the organization, write a letter to the editor of your town newspaper, or host a yard sale to raise money.

Become a Lifelong Hadassah Member

Hadassah, the Women's Zionist Organization of America, was founded in 1912 by Henrietta Szold and continues its groundbreaking work in health care, education, youth institutions, and land development to meet Israel's needs today. If you become a member, you not only support Israel, but also benefit from enrichment programs in the United States. For a donation of $360, you can become a member for life or give someone else the gift of membership. Think about your talents as you brainstorm ways to earn the $360. Could you host a soccer clinic for younger children? Bake desserts to sell to neighbors to serve at Thanksgiving or any of the Jewish holidays? Rake leaves, babysit, shovel snow, or wash cars?

✓ Get It Going

Go to www.hadassah.org to learn about all the amazing work Hadassah does. Here's a short description of one incredible initiative, the Hadassah Youth Aliyah villages, originally designed to rescue refugees from Nazi Germany. Today, many of the youth participating come from Ethiopia and the former Soviet Union as well as from homes in Israel with significant problems. From Hebrew language lessons and classes on Jewish heritage to athletic opportunities, art programs, and psychological support, Youth Aliyah students get the extra help and attention they need to become productive members of Israeli society.

Keep the Water Flowing

Fresh, drinkable water is a precious resource everywhere in the world, but especially in Israel, where the usable water supply is not sufficient to support the country's needs. The Jewish National Fund (JNF) is building reservoirs, exploring new water sources, implementing new agricultural techniques, and promoting conservation education to help solve the problem. You can raise money to support JNF's water supply initiatives by selling water at school and town sporting events while encouraging earth-friendly behavior at the same time. Bring large jugs of purified tap water to sell. Charge less for filling someone's reusable water bottle and more for water in a biodegradable cup you supply.

✓ Get It Going

To learn more about Israel's freshwater needs and see what your funds can accomplish, visit www.jnf.org/work-we-do/our-projects/water. If you raise $96, you will supply water for one person for one year; $384, a family of four; $1,140, a classroom of thirty children; $4,800, an army base of fifty soldiers.

Keep Israel Green by Going Green

With a population of 6.5 million growing in a country about the size of New Jersey, Israel's open space is precious. The Society for the Protection of Nature in Israel (SPNI; www.aspni.org) searches for environmentally sustainable and economically sound ways to promote growth while protecting Israel's unique environmental heritage. Why not start a bottle return/recycling service for your family and neighbors and make weekly collections of returnable glass and plastic bottles? The nickels or dimes you earn will add up to a sizable donation if you keep at it.

✓ Get It Going

To kick off your recycling service, send an e-mail to neighbors explaining your project with a link to the work SPNI does. Remember to specify the date, time, and frequency of your pick-ups, and ask neighbors to suggest a convenient pick-up location for their bottles.

Real Kids, Real Mitzvot

Rebecca G.—Nurturing a Connection to Israel

Sisterhood of the traveling letters: Rebecca's temple has a sister congregation in Haifa, Israel, and Rebecca corresponded with a thirteen-year-old Israeli girl there. For her mitzvah project, Rebecca wanted to broaden her connection to her sister congregation and to Israel in general. Rebecca raised money by organizing bake sales at her temple for Bar and Bat Mitzvah students in Haifa who were much less fortunate than herself.

Brotherhood of B'nai Mitzvah: With the money she raised, Rebecca purchased *kippot* and *Kiddush* cups for the B'nai Mitzvah students in her sister congregation. But Rebecca's commitment to Israel did not stop with her Bat Mitzvah. The year after, she hosted a teenager from Israel, who stayed with her and her family during Yom Kippur. Even four years after her Bat Mitzvah, Rebecca deepened her connection to Israel by enrolling in Hebrew classes to learn the language spoken in Israel.

Gabriel R. and Harrison G.—Creating a Dream B-Ball Court for a Kibbutz

Shooting hoops: Machanayim is a small kibbutz in northern Israel that Gabriel visits when his family travels to Israel to see relatives. After school, the kibbutz is full of kids running around, happily playing games and sports, including Gabe's favorite sport, basketball. On his last visit, Gabe couldn't help but notice the state of disrepair of the basketball court on the kibbutz—complete with potholes, cracked cement, and leaning hoops.

Aiming high: Once he got home to the United States, Gabe realized how lucky he was to have really nice basketball courts right in his own neighborhood. Gabe wanted his Israeli friends to have high-quality courts, too, so he and his basketball buddy Harrison joined together to raise $3,000 to rebuild the kibbutz's court. The boys created a fund-raising flyer, complete with photos of the existing court and the court of their dreams. They approached fellow basketball-loving friends, family, and neighbors to donate. Kids helping kids … now that's truly a slam dunk.

Diana C.—Helping Israeli Kids Celebrate

Let's party: Diana loves parties—anytime, anywhere, and for any reason, including Purim, Hanukkah, and, of course, birthdays. When Diana learned that birthday parties are an unaffordable luxury to thousands of Israeli children, she wanted to do something to help. Her mom told her about the birthday party project of Birthday Angels in Israel (www.birthday-angels.org), an organization whose goal is to provide birthday celebrations for needy kids.

Party animals: Diana decided to sell something to raise money for Birthday Angels. She bought small rubber ducks wearing party hats for about a quarter apiece. She put them in clear bags with labels explaining the Birthday Angel program. She sold the ducks to family and friends for $5 apiece and raised almost $1,000. Diana donated all the money she raised to Birthday Angels for birthday parties. Diana explains her joy at bringing joy to others: "I really had fun telling my friends about the work of Birthday Angels, and I loved reading the thank-you cards from the kids who had parties with my donation."

Izzy L.—Care Package Creator

Everyone loves care packages: Especially Izzy while she is at overnight camp. But, on a family trip to Israel, Izzy visited the Mount Herzl Military Cemetery in Jerusalem and learned about the non-Israeli soldiers who have died defending Israel. This visit had such a profound impact on her that Izzy decided to support Israeli soldiers for her mitzvah project.

Including Israeli soldiers: Izzy learned about A Package From Home (www.apackagefromhome.org), a group that creates and delivers care packages to soldiers in the Israeli Defense Forces who do not have family in Israel or who have been severely wounded and are in long-term care. Izzy ran bake sales and craft sales to raise enough money to "adopt" a troop. She enlisted her friends to help her with the cooking and the creation of jewelry made from recycled materials to make sure each soldier received a care package.

Israel Journal

The State of Israel was established on May 14, 1948 (5 Iyar 5708). It is a relatively young country, and your support can go a long way in helping it continue to flourish.

What inspired you in this chapter? Jot down ideas you want to remember for possible mitzvah projects … and beyond.

_____

_____

_____

_____

_____

_____

_____

_____

_____

_____

_____

_____

_____

_____

_____

_____

_____

_____

_____

_____

_____

Jewish Heritage

"Trust yourself. Create the kind of self that you will be happy to live with all of your life. Make the most of yourself by fanning the tiny inner sparks of possibility into flames of achievement."

—GOLDA MEIR (1898–1978), FOURTH PRIME MINISTER OF ISRAEL

Support Non-Jews Who Risked Their Lives for Jewish Ancestors

The Jewish Foundation for the Righteous (JFR) provides monthly financial assistance to more than nine hundred aged and needy non-Jews, called "Righteous Gentiles," who during the Holocaust risked their own lives, and likely the lives of their own families, to save Jews' lives. The support you provide through the JFR helps cover the cost of much-needed essentials, including food, home heating fuel, medical care, and medicine for the rest of these elders' lives. Righteous Gentiles reside in twenty-three countries, with the majority in Poland and other Eastern Europe countries. What an honor to help these brave and righteous persons in their time of need.

✓ Get It Going

The JFR offers a special Bar/Bat Mitzvah program that gives you the opportunity to choose a rescuer to support. The JFR calls this "twinning," and the minimum donation for the Twinning

Program is $180. By participating in the program, you perform the mitzvot of *tzedakah*, *tikkun olam*, and *hakarat hatov*. Find out more at the JFR website: www.jfr.org/site/PageServer.

Celebrate with Jewish Kids around the World

Maybe you live in a suburb or a city where there are many other Jewish families. Or perhaps you have to travel a distance to join other Jewish kids at Hebrew/Sunday school or a Jewish Community Center. But some Jews living around the world in countries such as Cuba, India, Cameroon, Suriname, and Poland are isolated. Even worse, some are ostracized from mainstream society. You can help Jewish children in small communities celebrate their Judaism simply by sending them items that make Jewish holidays more fun. Think about art projects, music, and holiday-specific items such as dreidels and instructions for playing the dreidel game for Hanukkah; masks, crayons, and *groggers* for Purim; and CDs of holiday songs.

✓ Get It Going

Locating isolated groups of Jewish kids is definitely a challenge, but a rewarding one once you succeed and establish a connection. Here is one approach: Start by searching for synagogues in major cities in a country that interests you, such as Kiev in the Ukraine. Contact the rabbi or educator by e-mail or mail, and explain that you would like to reach out to Jewish kids who are isolated from a sizable Jewish community and provide them with age-appropriate items to celebrate different Jewish holidays. It could be preschoolers or teens—the important thing is that you get connected to an adult who can be your bridge to children. Once you make a connection and know the age and number of kids, make sure your ideas are on track and that you follow through on your commitments. Hopefully you can establish an ongoing relationship and send packages a few times a year.

Honor Germans Who Keep Memories Alive of Jewish Life in Europe before Nazism

In 2000, the Obermayer German Jewish History Awards were established to honor non-Jewish Germans who work to preserve the memory of the history, culture, cemeteries, and synagogues of Jewish communities that existed in Germany before the Holocaust. These men and women volunteers educate people about the contribution Jews made to Germany, honor the memory of Jews who died, and rebuild connections between Jews and non-Jews. While these volunteers have devoted many hours to their projects, until recently few have been honored for their efforts. The German Jewish Community History Council encourages Jews all over the world to recognize these individuals and bring international attention to their activities. How can you help? Simply write thank-you notes to award winners for their efforts. You can even go a step further and write a report about an Obermayer Award winner for a history or an English paper. Find the names and stories of these unsung heroes at http://www.obermayer.us/award and choose a few that speak to you.

✓ Get It Going

Send your thank-you notes to Arthur S. Obermayer, President, Obermayer Foundation, Inc., 239 Chestnut Street, West Newton, MA 02465-2931, e-mail: obermayer@alum.mit.edu, so he can pass them along. Mr. Obermayer is a high-tech entrepreneur and philanthropist in the Boston, Massachusetts, area. He started the Jewish Museum in his ancestral German town of Creglingen, and recently a volume was published about his family, *The Obermayers: A History of a Jewish Family in Germany and America, 1618–2009*. Mr. Obermayer is also a board member of the American Jewish Historical Society (www.ajhs.org), and received from the German president the Bundesverdienstkreuz—the Cross of the Order of Merit—the highest tribute given by the Federal Republic of Germany.

Carry on Traditional Jewish Cooking

What special family recipes for Jewish foods do you love? Is it your grandmother's matzah ball and chicken soup, gefilte fish, or rugelach? How about your great-aunt's brisket or stuffed cabbage? While today we enjoy the ease of take-out, frozen, and packaged foods, it is important to make sure family recipes are passed along from generation to generation. So get on your apron, get out pen and paper, and follow a relative into the kitchen to help you prepare and record your family's traditional recipes. You're likely to learn about so much more than food. And then you'll be able to pass along family recipes and family history to your children, who hopefully will do the same for their children.

✓ Get It Going

Make sure to share whatever you end up learning to cook with others. You could offer your food for the *Oneg Shabbat* at your temple, provide food for local shelters, or bring dinner over to an elderly or ill neighbor.

Put Yiddish Words in Your *Kepele* (Sweet Little Head)

Oy vey! You don't know any Yiddish? Yiddish is a language that was spoken among millions of Ashkenazi Jews in Central and Eastern Europe before World War II. It has both German and Hebrew roots. The language was so widespread among Jewish immigrants to America that during the 1930s, the Yiddish newspaper *The Forward* had a U.S. circulation of over 250,000 readers nationwide. Yiddish is written with the Hebrew alphabet. Today, it is still spoken in some Orthodox communities worldwide, especially in Hasidic ones. There is also a wonderful legacy of Yiddish literature. The Jewish author who wrote under the pen name of "Sholem Aleichem" (1859–1916) wrote the story that inspired the Broadway musical and movie *Fiddler on the Roof*. You can help keep this language alive by learning Yiddish words and phrases and teaching other kids your new vocabulary.

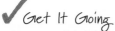 Get It Going

Many Yiddish words have found their way into American English. Have you ever heard someone say, "I'm tired of schlepping [dragging] these bags?" Or "I'm a bit of a klutz [clumsy person]?" Finding an actual Yiddish teacher might prove difficult, but don't despair. Perhaps you have family members or friends who can share their knowledge with you. Check out online resources or books to learn some words of this rich language. Keep a running list of your new vocabulary, and then you could make a poster of Yiddish words and phrases to share with your Hebrew class or write a short story that uses Yiddish expressions to share with family and friends.

Pass Along Your Knowledge of the Hebrew Alphabet

You are already very familiar with the twenty-two letters of the *aleph-bet*. You know that, unlike English, Hebrew is written from right to left and traditional Hebrew writing uses no vowels, only consonants. In some ways, Hebrew letters are not as complicated to recognize as the letters used in this very book. In Hebrew, there are no separate capital or lowercase letters. But to someone who has never gone to Hebrew school or had a Hebrew tutor, reading from the prayer book in synagogue can be intimidating. Maybe your mom or dad never studied Hebrew but would love to read the major prayers in Hebrew.

✓ Get It Going

Pull out your old Hebrew school workbooks or borrow some from your synagogue to use for lessons. You could also make flashcards and find fun *aleph-bet* songs on YouTube.com. If your prayer book is in Hebrew only, a great mitzvah would be to provide transliteration of an important prayer, such as the *Mi Sheberach*, the prayer for healing.

Real Kids, Real Mitzvot

Alana R. and Jackie B.—Cousins Connect to Kids in Their Grandfather's Homeland

A trip of a lifetime: Jackie and Alana's families joined their eighty-three-year-old grandfather on a trip back to his birthplace in Lviv, Poland, a town that is now part of the Ukraine, for his second Bar Mitzvah. A Holocaust survivor, he had fled Poland when he was only fourteen years old. On their trip, the cousins met preschool-aged Jewish children in their grandfather's town of Lviv and were struck by how sparse and austere the tiny classroom appeared.

Sending pride and joy: Back at home, the cousins met with the family educator at their own temple to learn about kids' activities for holiday celebrations. Over the year, they sent nine packages to the children's teacher in Lviv so that the boys and girls there could learn more about the Jewish holidays, decorate their classroom, and enjoy art projects and games. How did Alana and Jackie know their gifts were well received? They saw e-mail photos of smiling kids enjoying their projects.

Noah G.—Strengthening His Jewish Identity

Remembering: Remember Us: The Holocaust B'nai Mitzvah Project (www.remember-us.org) offers children preparing for their Bar/Bat Mitzvah the opportunity to connect with the memory of over one million children lost in the Holocaust before they could be called to the Torah. Noah was given the name of Pinkhas Gabel, and his journey in learning about this boy strengthened Noah's connection to his Jewish heritage and his good fortune in becoming a Bar Mitzvah.

In his own words: Noah's Torah portion was about loving the stranger as yourself.

"I didn't know what it meant to love the stranger as myself before I started studying for my Bar Mitzvah. I hadn't given much thought to how it applied to people I didn't really know. And like most kids, I really only had to think about myself. But then I found out about Pinkhas Gabel. Pinkhas was born in 1934 in a town called Myszkow in Poland. His mother's name was Feigel; his father's name was Yaakov. Pinkhas was in Birkenau concentration camp during the Shoah, or the Holocaust. I don't know anything more about him, since he died there in 1943. He was nine years old. I became connected with Pinkhas through Remember Us: The Holocaust B'nai Mitzvah Project. Knowing about Pinkhas made me realize how lucky I am just to be alive. Loving Pinkhas as I love myself means that I will celebrate this day in his name, and honor his memory."

Jenna S.—Millions to Remember

Encouraging tolerance: Even though Jenna's family has no personal connection to the Holocaust, she often read books on the subject and once heard Elie Wiesel, the great Nobel Prize–winning author, talk about the Shoah. Jenna felt that the Holocaust started because people learned to hate others different from themselves. So, for her project, she set out to accomplish two goals: first, to raise six million pennies, one for each Jewish life lost in the Holocaust; and two, to increase awareness about the importance of tolerance.

Changing the world with change: Undaunted by her huge target, Jenna researched groups on the Internet and decided to donate all the pennies—and checks—she collected to the Simon Wiesenthal Center (www.wiesenthal.com), an organization that fights anti-Semitism, focuses on lessons of the Holocaust, and promotes respect for and tolerance of all people through its Museum of Tolerance in Los Angeles (www.museumoftolerance.com). Jenna got the word out about the penny collection through e-mails, letters to corporations, newspaper articles, and television coverage. With the help of family, friends, and the community, she amassed 800,000 pennies—$8,000. Jenna remembered one special contributor: "A man, who wasn't Jewish, read about my mitzvah project in our local paper. He had been collecting pennies for thirty years, more than twice as long as my whole life. He was so generous. He donated all those coins to my mitzvah project!"

Jewish Heritage Journal

Honor your Jewish past and future all at once with
your mitzvah project.

What inspired you in this chapter? Jot down ideas you want to
remember for possible mitzvah projects ... and beyond.

_____

_____

_____

_____

_____

_____

_____

_____

_____

_____

_____

_____

_____

_____

_____

_____

_____

_____

_____

_____

Everyday Mitzvot

Eighteen Small Ideas That Are Big

Think of your Bar/Bat Mitzvah mitzvah project as a beginning, not an end, to the good you can do in the world. Small everyday efforts are just as important as big ones. In fact, small efforts add up to great change. Read through these eighteen everyday mitzvot ideas to see how easy it is to make the world a better place—one interaction at a time.

Why eighteen projects? The Hebrew word for "life" is *chai*, and the numerical values of the Hebrew letters for *chai* together equal eighteen. Think of these eighteen projects as symbolic of making mitzvot a way of life.

1. Fend for Your Four-Legged Friend

Remember when you begged your parents, "Please, please, please can we get a dog? I promise I'll take care of it." While your intentions were good, it's likely your mom or dad does most of the pet care. Make a point of offering to take your dog out for a walk, brush his or her coat, or fill the water bowl … *before* you're asked.

2. Get One, Give One

Every time you get a new shirt, pants, or sweater, why not donate one you've outgrown? Start collecting clothing to give to kids in need. Once you've gathered a pile, find a local or national agency that collects used clothes. You could even check to see if there is a Hadassah Thrift Shop in your area.

3. Double the Bins—Half the Trash

Paper is the biggest source of household waste, yet only a fraction of it is recycled. Instead of sending paper trash to the landfill, put an extra trash bin wherever you do homework for all your discarded paper. Yes, two bins are better than one!

4. Bring on the Bagels

Surprise your mom and dad with breakfast in bed one weekend morning when they least expect it. Don't wait for Mother's Day or Father's Day. They'll love waking up to the sweet smell of your breakfast treat.

5. Wrap It Up in Laughter

You've selected the perfect birthday gift and it's time to wrap it. Share a little laughter by covering the present with the colorful Sunday comics. It's a perfect way to "reuse"—one of the three "Rs" of conservation: reduce, recycle, reuse.

6. Wake Up and Toss the Paper

Are you half asleep as you head out to meet the school bus in the morning? Here's a way to wake up and brighten your neighbors' mornings, too. As you pass each house, look for the newspaper and run it up or toss it up to your neighbor's front steps. You won't make the news, but you will make someone's day get off to a pleasant start.

7. Pass Along Your Favorite Books

After you finish a great book, why not share it with others? Pass it along to a reluctant reader, to your classroom library, to your public library, or to a neighbor or relative—even an adult. Adults often enjoy youth fiction and nonfiction books as well. If the book you finished was a library book, then send an e-mail letting people know about the book and why you loved it.

8. Unplug It

Yes, we all know it's important to turn off electronics when not using them, but did you know that you can further reduce your carbon footprint by unplugging your cell phone charger, curling iron, or computer when you're not using it? They use power just by being connected to an electrical outlet.

9. Ease the Pain

It's inevitable—one of your friends is going to have a sports injury and have to be sidelined. To help ease the pain, how about suggesting to the coach that the team dedicate the next game to him or her, start games with a cheer in your teammate's honor, or invite your friend to be scorekeeper?

10. Eat Your Vegetables ... and Grains ... and Fruits

Enjoy your spaghetti, but hold the meatballs. Substitute plant-based foods for meats a couple of times a week. It's good not just for you, but for the Earth, too. In fact, it takes about ten pounds of plants to produce just one pound of meat!

11. Keep Current on Israel

The Red Sea parting, Haman's plot, the victory of the Maccabees—that's ancient history! What's happening in Israel today? Find out at www.jerusalempost.com. Whether its knishes or the Knesset, checking out this website keeps you informed.

12. Lessen Loneliness

Next time you are choosing teammates or getting a group together for a class project, reach out to someone new or someone who doesn't get asked very often to join in. Is there an exchange student or a shy classmate you could approach? Embrace inclusion over exclusion. You may just make a new friend, too.

13. Stay Connected

You know how much your grandparents love to hear about what's going on in your life. With everyone's busy schedules, speaking on the phone can be a challenge. Next time you're face-to-face with your *bubbe* and *zayde,* teach them how to use e-mail or text messaging as a quick way to stay in touch. Remember to explain e-mail "lingo" like TTYL, LOL, LYL.

14. Waste Not, Want Not

Tired of your old T-shirts, but they fit just fine? There are ways to turn frumpy into funky and not be wasteful. One idea is to redesign them. First, cut the side seams of a T-shirt up to the armpits, next cut one-inch-thick fringe along the sides, then tie the fringe all the way up. Another idea is to pull out those fabric markers and write inspirational words all over your T. Or create your own style makeover idea.

15. Thank a Teacher

The start of the new year in January is the perfect time to show appreciation to your teachers. As corny as it might feel to you, it really means a lot to them. A handmade cartoon, origami snowflake, haiku, or just a heartfelt note all make the grade.

16. Make a Little Music

One of your friends a little down? Maybe he's sick and missing school. Maybe she's struggling with math. Or perhaps it's not making the team that's making them blue. Send along a personalized playlist of upbeat tunes. It's sure to lift anyone's spirits.

17. (Re)gift

What do you do with a gift you don't want? Instead of putting it in the back of your closet, donate it to a kid in need. Or, instead of exchanging the gift for something else for yourself, return it and buy a gift for someone who would really appreciate something special. You know the saying, "It's better to give than to receive."

18. Pray for Peace

Shabbat begins with a greeting of peace, and the Shabbat morning service ends with the *Oseh Shalom* prayer for peace: "God who makes peace in High Places, God will make peace for us and for all Israel, and let us say, Amen." When you have a quiet moment, you could recite this prayer or craft your own personal one.

Authors' Note

This is a book about inspiring young people to create meaningful Bar and Bat Mitzvah mitzvah projects. Yet, it was actually Mitzvah Day that inspired us to write this book.

Have you ever participated in Mitzvah Day? Then you've felt the power of kids, parents, and grandparents going out into the community to help where help is needed. Preparing meals for the hungry, cleaning up parks, and painting community centers are just a few of the ways people reach out during this day of service.

Mitzvah Day was launched in 1991 under the leadership of Rabbi Bruce Lustig and members of Washington Hebrew Congregation in D.C. Since then, many synagogues across the country have hosted Mitzvah Days, organizing volunteers to improve the lives of people in their communities. But, the intent of Mitzvah Day is more than just a once-a-year event. It encourages an everyday commitment to Judaism's teaching of *tikkun olam*, "repairing the world."

We hope our book helps families extend the spirit of Mitzvah Day throughout the year, especially as young adults prepare for their Bar or Bat Mitzvah. Young adulthood is a great time for B'nai Mitzvah to feel how their energy and enthusiasm can truly make a difference. Mitzvah projects remind us to help those less fortunate, respect the planet, be good citizens, support Israel in its quest for security and peace, insist on honesty and integrity, and just be kind … all to make the world a better place.

In honor of our clergy, we are donating a portion of the proceeds of this book to charities of their choice.

Diane Heiman
member, Washington Hebrew Congregation, Washington, D.C.
Liz Suneby
member, Temple Beth Elohim, Wellesley, Massachusetts

"LOL" Glossary

If your *Bubbe* and *Zayde* are trying to get you and your friends to contribute to a *tzedakah* fund by selling knishes under the sukkah, then you'll definitely want to read this glossary to find out what they are talking about!

aleph-bet: The Hebrew alphabet, written right to left.

Ashkenazim: Jews who descend from ancestors who lived in Central and Eastern Europe.

ba'al tekiah: The person (with big lungs) who blows the ram's horn or shofar in synagogue during Rosh Hashanah and Yom Kippur. *Ba'al tekiah* means "master of the blast."

Bar/Bat Mitzvah: OK, if you're reading this book, you're likely living these words. But here's the literal translation: "son or daughter of the commandments." The plural of Bar Mitzvah is B'nai Mitzvah, and the plural of Bat Mitzvah is B'not Mitzvah.

bimah: That's the elevated part of the sanctuary you go up to when you read from the Torah.

B'nai Mitzvah: See **Bar/Bat Mitzvah**.

bubbe: Different families have different names for *grandma*. Some say "nana;" others, "grammie" or *oma*. Do you call your grandma *bubbe*? That's Yiddish for "grandma."

cantor: A cantor, or *chazzan* in Hebrew, is the person responsible for the musical parts of synagogue services. Can you imagine Shabbat services without the beauty of music and song?

chai: The meaning of the Hebrew word *chai* is "life." This word is central to Jewish culture in many ways. Have you ever heard the toast *l'chayyim*—to life—at a Jewish event? The numerical value of the Hebrew letters that spell *chai* equals eighteen, a symbolic number for good luck in Jewish tradition.

challah: What's Shabbat without a delicious loaf of challah? Challah is sweet Jewish bread made with eggs and often braided.

Chanukah: See **Hanukkah**.

chatchkie: Knickknack. The literal meaning of this Yiddish word is "a dust-collecting item."

chuppah: The canopy under which the bride and groom stand during a Jewish wedding ceremony, symbolizing the home the couple will build together. Sometimes the cloth of a *chuppah* is a *tallit,* so take good care of the *tallit* you wear at your Bar/Bat Mitzvah. It may come in handy in your future!

dreidel: A four-sided top with a letter of the Hebrew alphabet on each side: *nun, gimel, hei,* and *shin.* These letters form the acronym for *Nes gadol hayah sham,* "A great miracle happened there." The letters also form a mnemonic for the rules of game often played at Hanukkah celebrations: *nun* stands for the Yiddish word *nite,* meaning "nothing"; *hei* for *halb,* meaning "half"; *gimel* for *gants,* meaning "all"; and *shin* for *shteln,* meaning "put."

erev: Hebrew for "the day before" or "the eve of"; for example, Erev Pesach is the day before Passover; Erev Shabbat is Friday night.

etz chaim: Hebrew for "tree of life," an image used in Judaism as well as in many religions and cultures that expresses the unity of life on earth. The Torah is often referred to as "a Tree of Life" because it is a guide to proper behavior.

gefilte fish: Think of this traditional Jewish food as a fish hamburger that you eat cold!

gemilut hasadim: Hebrew for "acts of loving-kindness." Jewish tradition tells us that the world stands on three pillars: Torah, worship, and acts of loving-kindness.

grogger: A noisemaker used at Purim to drown out evil Haman's name. Costumes, singing, dancing, and lots of noise—what could be more fun!

hachnasat orchim: The mitzvah of welcoming strangers.

Hadassah: Nearly one hundred years ago, an American Jewish scholar and activist named Henrietta Szold founded this American women's organization to support Judaism, Israel, and American ideals. Focusing on education and health, Hadassah makes the world a better place.

hakarat hatov: What better way to focus on the positive in the world than to seek out and recognize goodness? That is the meaning of *hakarat hatov.*

Haman: An advisor to the king of Persia who tried to exterminate the Jewish people in about 355 BCE. Remember, he's the guy with the three-cornered hat.

hamantaschen: Triangle-shaped pastries, served at Purim, that mimic the three-cornered hat worn by Haman.

Hanukkah: The eight-day Festival of Lights commemorating the victory of the Jewish people over the Syrian Greeks in 165 BCE and the rededication of the Second Temple in Jerusalem. It is often spelled "Hanukah" or "Chanukah" or "Chanuka." No matter how you choose to spell it, just remember to eat lots of potato latkes or doughnuts fried in oil.

Hasidic: Referring to a branch of Orthodox Judaism founded in Poland in the 1700s that emphasizes mysticism, joy, and prayer.

HaTikvah: The Israeli national anthem lyrics were written in 1886 by Naphtali Herz Imber, an English poet originally from Bohemia. The melody was composed by Samuel Cohen from Moldavia.

Hava Nagila: If you've ever been to a Bar/Bat Mitzvah or a Jewish wedding, you've undoubtedly heard *Hava Nagila*, the Hebrew folk song, played when you dance the hora! *Hava Nagila* means "Let's Rejoice." How fitting!

hora: A circle dance often danced to the music of *Hava Nagila.* This popular Israeli folk dance is a staple at Jewish celebrations in the United States and Canada, too. Be prepared at your Bar or Bat Mitzvah to be lifted up on a chair in the middle of the circle of dancers!

kepele: Yiddish for head: "Put a hat on your *kepele."*

Kiddush: The special blessing recited over wine or grape juice on Shabbat and Jewish holidays.

Kiddush **cup:** A silver goblet is often used to hold the wine for *Kiddush,* although any cup will do!

kippot: Plural of *kippah.* A *kippah* or *yarmulke* is a skullcap tradition-ally worn all the time by ritually observant Jewish men, and worn at synagogue by both men and women in Conservative and many Reform communities.

klezmer: The traditional music of the Ashkenazi Jews of Eastern Europe. Klezmer melodies are very expressive—you'd never mistake them for calming lullabies!

klutz: The person who trips over his or her own feet.

Knesset: The Parliament, or legislative branch, of the Israeli gov-ernment.

knish: A Jewish appetizer or snack made with a shell of dough and typically filled with mashed potato or meat. It's a Yiddish word and if you have hunger pangs at the deli, ask for a Ka-NISH.

ma'asim tovim: The Hebrew way to say "good deeds."

Maccabees: Who led the rebellion in the second century BCE against an empire that forced Jews to worship Greek gods? The family of Mattathias, known as the Maccabees.

matzah: Unleavened bread eaten at Passover. Many people love when matzah is made into matzah balls for chicken soup.

Megillah: The biblical book of Esther, which commemorates the story of how a plot to kill all the Jewish people in ancient Persia was foiled by a brave Jewish woman, her cousin Mordechai, and King Ahasuerus.

mensch: It's Yiddish for "a decent, admirable person." Today we'd call that person "a good guy."

Mi Sheberach: A prayer for physical and spiritual healing.

mishloach manot: Food baskets that are given as gifts during Purim.

mishpachah: The Yiddish word for "family," as in the expression "the whole *mishpachah.*"

mitzvah: Literally speaking, "mitzvah" means "commandment of the Jewish law." We use the word to mean "a good deed."

Mitzvah Day: An annual congregation-wide day of community service. Think of it as your mitzvah project times one hundred! It was started in 1991 by Rabbi Bruce Lustig at Washington Hebrew Congregation and is now held in hundreds of congregations.

Oneg Shabbat: Oneg Shabbat literally means "pleasure of Shabbat," but today people use it to refer to a small meal after Shabbat services on Friday evening or Saturday morning.

oy vey: "Oh, no" in Yiddish, as in "*Oy vey,* I only have three months left to learn my Torah portion."

pikuach nefesh: Saving a life—the ultimate mitzvah.

pushke: Yiddish for *tzedakah* box.

rabbi: Very simply, "rabbi" means "Torah teacher."

Rosh Hashanah: The Jewish New Year.

rugelach: Crescent-shaped pastries with raisins, walnuts, cinnamon, chocolate, marzipan, poppy seeds, or jam rolled up inside. Bet you can't eat just one!

schlep: "To drag" in Yiddish. Do you schlep your body to school early in the morning?

Shabbat: Sabbath, the day of rest after God finished the work of creating the universe.

shevarim: The three medium wailing sounds from the shofar.

Shoah: The Holocaust, the murder of approximately six million European Jews during World War II by Nazi Germany and others.

shpiel: Plays put on in celebration of Purim are called *shpiels.* They take all shapes and forms, from short funny monologues to puppet shows to elaborate plays. Whatever their format, Purim *shpiels* are a Jewish tradition.

sukkah: A temporary shelter made during the biblical holiday of Sukkot, the holiday that commemorates God helping the Jews as they wandered for forty years in the desert and celebrates the final harvest of the year.

tallit: A Jewish prayer shawl. The plural of *tallit* in Hebrew is *tallitot.*

Talmud: The Talmud is a record of ancient rabbis' discussions about Jewish laws, ethics, customs, and history.

tekiah: The one long blast from the shofar.

teruah: The nine fast blasts, one after another, from the shofar.

tikkun olam: The literal Hebrew translation is "world repair." This phrase has come to mean the pursuit of social justice for all people.

tokea: The person who blows the ram's horn or shofar in synagogue during the High Holy Days.

Torah: The teachings of Judaism given to the Jews by God at Mount Sinai. It is the Five Books of Moses: Genesis, Exodus, Leviticus, Numbers, and Deuteronomy.

Tu B'Shevat: This holiday celebrates the New Year for trees. Traditionally, people celebrate the holiday outdoors, planting trees, eating fruit, and singing songs about trees.

tzedakah: The word *tzedakah* is commonly translated as "charity," but literally means "justice, righteousness, and fairness." During the High Holy Days, we learn that repentance, prayer, and *tzedakah* are the ways to gain God's forgiveness from our sins.

tzitzit: This word has such a wonderful sound, you'll likely be saying it just for the fun of it. But, so you know what you are saying, *tzitzit* are the fringes attached to the four corners of the prayer shawl (*tallit*).

Yiddish: Yiddish is a language based on German with many Hebrew phrases and words from other countries in which Jewish people lived woven into it. Although it isn't connected to one country, for many years it was the primary language of Jews from Central and Eastern Europe. It is an onomatopoetic language. That means lots of words sound just like their meaning. Ever had to schlep your backpack upstairs?

Yom Kippur: This holiday, known as the Day of Atonement, is the holiest day of the year for Jewish people. Many adult Jews fast as well as pray as part of the Yom Kippur observance.

zayde, zeyde, zadie, zaideh, **or** *zaideh:* No matter how you spell it, pronounced *zay-dee,* it means "grandpa" in Yiddish. As in, "Don't blame me. I didn't do it! Just ask my *Zayde*!"

Suggestions for Further Reading

Adelman, Penina, Ali Feldman, and Shulamit Reinharz. *The JGirl's Guide: The Young Jewish Woman's Handbook for Coming of Age*. Woodstock, VT: Jewish Lights, 2005.

Feinstein, Edward. *Tough Questions Jews Ask: A Young Adult's Guide to Building a Jewish Life*, 2nd ed. Woodstock, VT: Jewish Lights, 2011.

Jacobs, Jill. *Where Justice Dwells: A Hands-On Guide to Doing Social Justice in Your Jewish Community*. Woodstock, VT: Jewish Lights, 2011.

Leneman, Helen, ed. *Bar/Bat Mitzvah Basics: A Family Guide to Coming of Age Together*, 2nd ed. Woodstock, VT: Jewish Lights, 2001.

Pearl, Judea, and Ruth Pearl, eds. *I Am Jewish: Personal Reflections Inspired by the Last Words of Daniel Pearl*. Woodstock, VT: Jewish Lights, 2004.

Salkin, Jeffrey K. "Bar and Bat Mitzvah's Meaning: Preparing Spiritually with Your Child. *LifeLights* pamphlet. Woodstock, VT: Jewish Lights, 2006.

———. *For Kids—Putting God on Your Guest List: How to Claim the Spiritual Meaning of Your Bar or Bat Mitzvah*, 2nd ed. Woodstock, VT: Jewish Lights, 2007.

———. *Putting God on the Guest List: How to Reclaim the Spiritual Meaning of Your Child's Bar or Bat Mitzvah*, 3rd ed. Woodstock, VT: Jewish Lights, 2005.

Salkin Jeffrey K., and Nina Salkin. *The Bar/Bat Mitzvah Memory Book: An Album for Treasuring the Spiritual Celebration*, 2nd ed. Woodstock, VT: Jewish Lights, 2006.

Schwarz, Sidney. *Judaism Justice: The Jewish Passion to Repair the World*. Woodstock, VT: Jewish Lights, 2008.

Spirituality/Prayer

Making Prayer Real: Leading Jewish Spiritual Voices on Why Prayer Is Difficult and What to Do about It *By Rabbi Mike Comins*
A new and different response to the challenges of Jewish prayer, with "best prayer practices" from Jewish spiritual leaders of all denominations.
6 x 9, 320 pp, Quality PB, 978-1-58023-417-7 **$18.99**

Witnesses to the One: The Spiritual History of the *Sh'ma*
By Rabbi Joseph B. Meszler; Foreword by Rabbi Elyse Goldstein
6 x 9, 176 pp, Quality PB, 978-1-58023-400-9 **$16.99**; HC, 978-1-58023-309-5 **$19.99**

My People's Prayer Book Series: Traditional Prayers, Modern Commentaries *Edited by Rabbi Lawrence A. Hoffman, PhD*
Provides diverse and exciting commentary to the traditional liturgy. Will help you find new wisdom in Jewish prayer, and bring liturgy into your life. Each book

includes Hebrew text, modern translations and commentaries from all perspectives of the Jewish world.
Vol. 1—The *Sh'ma* and Its Blessings
  7 x 10, 168 pp, HC, 978-1-879045-79-8 **$29.99**
Vol. 2—The *Amidah* 7 x 10, 240 pp, HC, 978-1-879045-80-4 **$24.95**
Vol. 3—*P'sukei D'zimrah* (Morning Psalms)
  7 x 10, 240 pp, HC, 978-1-879045-81-1 **$29.99**
Vol. 4—*Seder K'riat Hatorah* (The Torah Service)
  7 x 10, 264 pp, HC, 978-1-879045-82-8 **$29.99**
Vol. 5—*Birkhot Hashachar* (Morning Blessings)
  7 x 10, 240 pp, HC, 978-1-879045-83-5 **$24.95**
Vol. 6—*Tachanun* and Concluding Prayers
  7 x 10, 240 pp, HC, 978-1-879045-84-2 **$24.95**
Vol. 7—Shabbat at Home 7 x 10, 240 pp, HC, 978-1-879045-85-9 **$24.95**
Vol. 8—*Kabbalat Shabbat* (Welcoming Shabbat in the Synagogue)
  7 x 10, 240 pp, HC, 978-1-58023-121-3 **$24.99**
Vol. 9—Welcoming the Night: *Minchah* and *Ma'ariv* (Afternoon and
  Evening Prayer) 7 x 10, 272 pp, HC, 978-1-58023-262-3 **$24.99**
Vol. 10—Shabbat Morning: *Shacharit* and *Musaf* (Morning and
  Additional Services) 7 x 10, 240 pp, HC, 978-1-58023-240-1 **$29.99**

Spirituality/Lawrence Kushner

I'm God; You're Not: Observations on Organized Religion & Other Disguises of the Ego
6 x 9, 256 pp, HC, 978-1-58023-441-2 **$21.99**

The Book of Letters: A Mystical Hebrew Alphabet
Popular HC Edition, 6 x 9, 80 pp, 2-color text, 978-1-879045-00-2 **$24.95**
Collector's Limited Edition, 9 x 12, 80 pp, gold-foil-embossed pages, w/ limited-edition silkscreened print, 978-1-879045-04-0 **$349.00**

The Book of Miracles: A Young Person's Guide to Jewish Spiritual Awareness
6 x 9, 96 pp, 2-color illus., HC, 978-1-879045-78-1 **$16.95** *For ages 9–13*

The Book of Words: Talking Spiritual Life, Living Spiritual Talk
6 x 9, 160 pp, Quality PB, 978-1-58023-020-9 **$18.99**

Eyes Remade for Wonder: A Lawrence Kushner Reader *Introduction by Thomas Moore*
6 x 9, 240 pp, Quality PB, 978-1-58023-042-1 **$18.95**

God Was in This Place & I, i Did Not Know: Finding Self, Spirituality and Ultimate Meaning 6 x 9, 192 pp, Quality PB, 978-1-879045-33-0 **$16.95**

Honey from the Rock: An Introduction to Jewish Mysticism
6 x 9, 176 pp, Quality PB, 978-1-58023-073-5 **$16.95**

Invisible Lines of Connection: Sacred Stories of the Ordinary
5½ x 8½, 160 pp, Quality PB, 978-1-879045-98-9 **$15.95**

Jewish Spirituality: A Brief Introduction for Christians
5½ x 8½, 112 pp, Quality PB, 978-1-58023-150-3 **$12.95**

The River of Light: Jewish Mystical Awareness
6 x 9, 192 pp, Quality PB, 978-1-58023-096-4 **$16.95**

The Way Into Jewish Mystical Tradition
6 x 9, 224 pp, Quality PB, 978-1-58023-200-5 **$18.99**; HC, 978-1-58023-029-2 **$21.95**

Judaism / Christianity / Interfaith

Christians & Jews—Faith to Faith: Tragic History, Promising Present, Fragile Future *By Rabbi James Rudin*
A probing examination of Christian-Jewish relations that looks at the major issues facing both faith communities. 6 x 9, 288 pp, HC, 978-1-58023-432-0 **$24.99**

How to Do Good & Avoid Evil: A Global Ethic from the Sources of Judaism *By Hans Küng and Rabbi Walter Homolka* Explores how the principles of Judaism provide the ethical norms for all religions to work together toward a more peaceful humankind. 6 x 9, 224 pp, HC, 978-1-59473-255-3 **$19.99***

Getting to the Heart of Interfaith: The Eye-Opening, Hope-Filled Friendship of a Pastor, a Rabbi and a Sheikh
By Rabbi Ted Falcon, Pastor Don Mackenzie and Imam Jamal Rahman
Presents ways we can work together to transcend the differences that have divided us historically. 6 x 9, 192 pp, Quality PB, 978-1-59473-263-8 **$16.99***

Claiming Earth as Common Ground: The Ecological Crisis through the Lens of Faith *By Rabbi Andrea Cohen-Kiener* 6 x 9, 192 pp, Quality PB, 978-1-59473-261-4 **$16.99***

Modern Jews Engage the New Testament: Enhancing Jewish Well-Being in a Christian Environment *By Rabbi Michael J. Cook, PhD* 6 x 9, 416 pp, HC, 978-1-58023-313-2 **$29.99**

The Changing Christian World: A Brief Introduction for Jews
By Rabbi Leonard A. Schoolman 5½ x 8½, 176 pp, Quality PB, 978-1-58023-344-6 **$16.99**

Christians & Jews in Dialogue: Learning in the Presence of the Other
By Mary C. Boys and Sara S. Lee
6 x 9, 240 pp, Quality PB, 978-1-59473-254-6 **$18.99**; HC, 978-1-59473-144-0 **21.99***

Disaster Spiritual Care: Practical Clergy Responses to Community, Regional and National Tragedy *Edited by Rabbi Stephen B. Roberts, BCJC, and Rev. Willard W. C. Ashley Sr., DMin, DH*
6 x 9, 384 pp, HC, 978-1-59473-240-9 **$40.00***

Healing the Jewish-Christian Rift: Growing Beyond Our Wounded History
By Ron Miller and Laura Bernstein 6 x 9, 288 pp, Quality PB, 978-1-59473-139-6 **$18.99***

How to Be a Perfect Stranger, 5th Edition: The Essential Religious Etiquette
Handbook *Edited by Stuart M. Matlins and Arthur J. Magida*
6 x 9, 432 pp, Quality PB, 978-1-59473-294-2 **$19.99***

InterActive Faith: The Essential Interreligious Community-Building Handbook
Edited by Rev. Bud Heckman with Rori Picker Neiss
6 x 9, 304 pp, Quality PB, 978-1-59473-273-7 **$16.99**; HC, 978-1-59473-237-9 **$29.99***

Introducing My Faith and My Community
The Jewish Outreach Institute Guide for the Christian in a Jewish Interfaith Relationship
By Rabbi Kerry M. Olitzky 6 x 9, 176 pp, Quality PB, 978-1-58023-192-3 **$16.99**

The Jewish Approach to Repairing the World (*Tikkun Olam*)
A Brief Introduction for Christians *By Rabbi Elliot N. Dorff, PhD, with Rev. Cory Willson*
5½ x 8½, 256 pp, Quality PB, 978-1-58023-349-1 **$16.99**

The Jewish Connection to Israel, the Promised Land: A Brief Introduction for Christians *By Rabbi Eugene Korn, PhD* 5½ x 8½, 192 pp, Quality PB, 978-1-58023-318-7 **$14.99**

Jewish Holidays: A Brief Introduction for Christians *By Rabbi Kerry M. Olitzky and Rabbi Daniel Judson* 5½ x 8½, 176 pp, Quality PB, 978-1-58023-302-6 **$16.99**

Jewish Ritual: A Brief Introduction for Christians *By Rabbi Kerry M. Olitzky and Rabbi Daniel Judson* 5½ x 8½, 144 pp, Quality PB, 978-1-58023-210-4 **$14.99**

A Jewish Understanding of the New Testament *By Rabbi Samuel Sandmel;
Preface by Rabbi David Sandmel* 5½ x 8½, 368 pp, Quality PB, 978-1-59473-048-1 **$19.99***

Righteous Gentiles in the Hebrew Bible: Ancient Role Models for Sacred
Relationships *By Rabbi Jeffrey K. Salkin; Foreword by Rabbi Harold M. Schulweis; Preface by Phyllis Tickle*
6 x 9, 192 pp, Quality PB, 978-1-58023-364-4 **$18.99**

Talking about God: Exploring the Meaning of Religious Life with Kierkegaard, Buber, Tillich and Heschel *By Rabbi Daniel F. Polish, PhD* 6 x 9, 160 pp, Quality PB, 978-1-59473-272-0 **$16.99***

We Jews and Jesus: Exploring Theological Differences for Mutual Understanding
By Rabbi Samuel Sandmel; Preface by Rabbi David Sandmel
6 x 9, 192 pp, Quality PB, 978-1-59473-208-9 **$16.99**

*A book from SkyLight Paths, Jewish Lights' sister imprint

Theology/Philosophy/The Way Into... Series

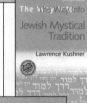

The Way Into… series offers an accessible and highly usable "guided tour" of the Jewish faith, people, history and beliefs—in total, an introduction to Judaism that will enable you to understand and interact with the sacred texts of the Jewish tradition. Each volume is written by a leading contemporary scholar and teacher, and explores one key aspect of Judaism. The Way Into… series enables all readers to achieve a real sense of Jewish cultural literacy through guided study.

The Way Into Encountering God in Judaism
By Rabbi Neil Gillman, PhD
For everyone who wants to understand how Jews have encountered God throughout history and today.
6 x 9, 240 pp, Quality PB, 978-1-58023-199-2 **$18.99**; HC, 978-1-58023-025-4 **$21.95**
Also Available: **The Jewish Approach to God:** A Brief Introduction for Christians
By Rabbi Neil Gillman, PhD
5½ x 8¼, 192 pp, Quality PB, 978-1-58023-190-9 **$16.95**

The Way Into Jewish Mystical Tradition
By Rabbi Lawrence Kushner
Allows readers to interact directly with the sacred mystical texts of the Jewish tradition. An accessible introduction to the concepts of Jewish mysticism, their religious and spiritual significance, and how they relate to life today.
6 x 9, 224 pp, Quality PB, 978-1-58023-200-5 **$18.99**; HC, 978-1-58023-029-2 **$21.95**

The Way Into Jewish Prayer
By Rabbi Lawrence A. Hoffman, PhD
Opens the door to 3,000 years of Jewish prayer, making anyone feel at home in the Jewish way of communicating with God.
6 x 9, 208 pp, Quality PB, 978-1-58023-201-2 **$18.99**

The Way Into Jewish Prayer Teacher's Guide
By Rabbi Jennifer Ossakow Goldsmith
8½ x 11, 42 pp, PB, 978-1-58023-345-3 **$8.99**
Download a free copy at www.jewishlights.com.

The Way Into Judaism and the Environment
By Jeremy Benstein, PhD
Explores the ways in which Judaism contributes to contemporary social-environmental issues, the extent to which Judaism is part of the problem and how it can be part of the solution.
6 x 9, 288 pp, Quality PB, 978-1-58023-368-2 **$18.99**

The Way Into Tikkun Olam (Repairing the World)
By Rabbi Elliot N. Dorff, PhD
An accessible introduction to the Jewish concept of the individual's responsibility to care for others and repair the world.
6 x 9, 304 pp, Quality PB, 978-1-58023-328-6 **$18.99**

The Way Into Torah
By Rabbi Norman J. Cohen, PhD
Helps guide you in the exploration of the origins and development of Torah, explains why it should be studied and how to do it.
6 x 9, 176 pp, Quality PB, 978-1-58023-198-5 **$16.99**

The Way Into the Varieties of Jewishness
By Sylvia Barack Fishman, PhD
Explores the religious and historical understanding of what it has meant to be Jewish from ancient times to the present controversy over "Who is a Jew?"
6 x 9, 288 pp, Quality PB, 978-1-58023-367-5 **$18.99**; HC, 978-1-58023-030-8 **$24.99**

Theology/Philosophy

The God Who Hates Lies: Confronting & Rethinking Jewish Tradition
By Dr. David Hartman with Charlie Buckholtz
The world's leading Modern Orthodox Jewish theologian probes the deepest questions at the heart of what it means to be a human being and a Jew.
6 x 9, 208 pp, HC, 978-1-58023-455-9 **$24.99**

Jewish Theology in Our Time: A New Generation Explores the
Foundations and Future of Jewish Belief *Edited by Rabbi Elliot J. Cosgrove, PhD;*
Foreword by Rabbi David J. Wolpe; Preface by Rabbi Carole B. Balin, PhD
A powerful and challenging examination of what Jews can believe—by a new generation's most dynamic and innovative thinkers.
6 x 9, 240 pp, HC, 978-1-58023-413-9 **$24.99**

Maimonides, Spinoza and Us: Toward an Intellectually Vibrant Judaism
By Rabbi Marc D. Angel, PhD A challenging look at two great Jewish philosophers and what their thinking means to our understanding of God, truth, revelation and reason. 6 x 9, 224 pp, HC, 978-1-58023-411-5 **$24.99**

The Death of Death: Resurrection and Immortality in Jewish Thought
By Rabbi Neil Gillman, PhD 6 x 9, 336 pp, Quality PB, 978-1-58023-081-0 **$18.95**

Doing Jewish Theology: God, Torah & Israel in Modern Judaism *By Rabbi Neil Gillman, PhD*
6 x 9, 304 pp, Quality PB, 978-1-58023-439-9 **$18.99**

Hasidic Tales: Annotated & Explained *Translation & Annotation by Rabbi Rami Shapiro*
5½ x 8½, 240 pp, Quality PB, 978-1-893361-86-7 **$16.95***

A Heart of Many Rooms: Celebrating the Many Voices within Judaism
By Dr. David Hartman 6 x 9, 352 pp, Quality PB, 978-1-58023-156-5 **$19.95**

The Hebrew Prophets: Selections Annotated & Explained
Translation & Annotation by Rabbi Rami Shapiro; Foreword by Rabbi Zalman M. Schachter-Shalomi
5½ x 8½, 224 pp, Quality PB, 978-1-59473-037-5 **$16.99***

A Jewish Understanding of the New Testament *By Rabbi Samuel Sandmel;*
Preface by Rabbi David Sandmel 5½ x 8½, 368 pp, Quality PB, 978-1-59473-048-1 **$19.99***

Jews and Judaism in the 21st Century: Human Responsibility, the Presence of God
and the Future of the Covenant *Edited by Rabbi Edward Feinstein; Foreword by Paula E. Hyman*
6 x 9, 192 pp, Quality PB, 978-1-58023-374-3 **$19.99**

A Living Covenant: The Innovative Spirit in Traditional Judaism
By Dr. David Hartman 6 x 9, 368 pp, Quality PB, 978-1-58023-011-7 **$25.00**

Love and Terror in the God Encounter: The Theological Legacy of Rabbi Joseph
B. Soloveitchik *By Dr. David Hartman* 6 x 9, 240 pp, Quality PB, 978-1-58023-176-3 **$19.95**

A Touch of the Sacred: A Theologian's Informal Guide to Jewish Belief
By Dr. Eugene B. Borowitz and Frances W. Schwartz
6 x 9, 256 pp, Quality PB, 978-1-58023-416-0 **$16.99**; HC, 978-1-58023-337-8 **$21.99**

Traces of God: Seeing God in Torah, History and Everyday Life *By Rabbi Neil Gillman, PhD*
6 x 9, 240 pp, Quality PB, 978-1-58023-369-9 **$16.99**

Your Word Is Fire: The Hasidic Masters on Contemplative Prayer
Edited and translated by Rabbi Arthur Green, PhD, and Barry W. Holtz
6 x 9, 160 pp, Quality PB, 978-1-879045-25-5 **$15.95**

I Am Jewish
Personal Reflections Inspired by the Last Words of Daniel Pearl
Almost 150 Jews—both famous and not—from all walks of life, from all around the world, write about many aspects of their Judaism.
Edited by Judea and Ruth Pearl 6 x 9, 304 pp, Deluxe PB w/ flaps, 978-1-58023-259-3 **$18.99**
Download a free copy of the *I Am Jewish Teacher's Guide* at www.jewishlights.com.
Hannah Senesh: Her Life and Diary, The First Complete Edition
By Hannah Senesh; Foreword by Marge Piercy; Preface by Eitan Senesh; Afterword by Roberta Grossman
6 x 9, 368 pp, b/w photos, Quality PB, 978-1-58023-342-2 **$19.99**

*A book from SkyLight Paths, Jewish Lights' sister imprint

Spirituality/Women's Interest

The Divine Feminine in Biblical Wisdom Literature: Selections Annotated & Explained *Translation & Annotation by Rabbi Rami Shapiro* 5½ x 8½, 240 pp, Quality PB, 978-1-59473-109-9 **$16.99** *(A book from SkyLight Paths, Jewish Lights' sister imprint)*

The Quotable Jewish Woman: Wisdom, Inspiration & Humor from the Mind & Heart *Edited by Elaine Bernstein Partnow* 6 x 9, 496 pp, Quality PB, 978-1-58023-236-4 **$19.99**

The Women's Haftarah Commentary: New Insights from Women Rabbis on the 54 Weekly Haftarah Portions, the 5 Megillot & Special Shabbatot *Edited by Rabbi Elyse Goldstein* 6 x 9, 560 pp, Quality PB, 978-1-58023-371-2 **$19.99**

The Women's Torah Commentary: New Insights from Women Rabbis on the 54 Weekly Torah Portions *Edited by Rabbi Elyse Goldstein* 6 x 9, 496 pp, Quality PB, 978-1-58023-370-5 **$19.99**; HC, 978-1-58023-076-6 **$34.95**

New Jewish Feminism: Probing the Past, Forging the Future *Edited by Rabbi Elyse Goldstein; Foreword by Anita Diamant* 6 x 9, 480 pp, Quality PB, 978-1-58023-448-1 **$19.99**; HC, 978-1-58023-359-0 **$24.99**

Spirituality/Crafts

(from SkyLight Paths, Jewish Lights' sister imprint)

Beading—The Creative Spirit: Finding Your Sacred Center through the Art of Beadwork *By Wendy Ellsworth* Invites you on a spiritual pilgrimage into the kaleidoscope world of glass and color. 7 x 9, 240 pp, 8-page full-color insert, b/w photos and diagrams, Quality PB, 978-1-59473-267-6 **$18.99**

Contemplative Crochet: A Hands-On Guide for Interlocking Faith and Craft *By Cindy Crandall-Frazier; Foreword by Linda Skolnik* Will take you on a path deeper into your crocheting and your spiritual awareness. 7 x 9, 208 pp, b/w photos, Quality PB, 978-1-59473-238-6 **$16.99**

The Knitting Way: A Guide to Spiritual Self-Discovery *By Linda Skolnik and Janice MacDaniels* Shows how to use knitting to strengthen your spiritual self. 7 x 9, 240 pp, b/w photos, Quality PB, 978-1-59473-079-5 **$16.99**

The Painting Path: Embodying Spiritual Discovery through Yoga, Brush and Color *By Linda Novick; Foreword by Richard Segalman* Explores the divine connection you can experience through art. 7 x 9, 208 pp, 8-page full-color insert, b/w photos, Quality PB, 978-1-59473-226-3 **$18.99**

The Quilting Path: A Guide to Spiritual Self-Discovery through Fabric, Thread and Kabbalah *By Louise Silk* Explores how to cultivate personal growth through quilt making. 7 x 9, 192 pp, b/w photos, Quality PB, 978-1-59473-206-5 **$16.99**

The Scrapbooking Journey: A Hands-On Guide to Spiritual Discovery *By Cory Richardson-Lauve; Foreword by Stacy Julian* Reveals how this craft can become a practice used to deepen and shape your life. 7 x 9, 176 pp, 8-page full-color insert, b/w photos, Quality PB, 978-1-59473-216-4 **$18.99**

Travel

Israel—A Spiritual Travel Guide, 2nd Edition: A Companion for the Modern Jewish Pilgrim *By Rabbi Lawrence A. Hoffman, PhD* 4¾ x 10, 256 pp, Illus., Quality PB, 978-1-58023-261-6 **$18.99**

Also Available: **The Israel Mission Leader's Guide** 5½ x 8½, 16 pp, PB, 978-1-58023-085-8 **$4.95**

Twelve Steps

100 Blessings Every Day: Daily Twelve Step Recovery Affirmations, Exercises for Personal Growth & Renewal Reflecting Seasons of the Jewish Year *By Rabbi Kerry M. Olitzky; Foreword by Rabbi Neil Gillman, PhD* 4½ x 6½, 432 pp, Quality PB, 978-1-879045-30-9 **$16.99**

Recovery from Codependence: A Jewish Twelve Steps Guide to Healing Your Soul *By Rabbi Kerry M. Olitzky* 6 x 9, 160 pp, Quality PB, 978-1-879045-32-3 **$13.95**

Twelve Jewish Steps to Recovery, 2nd Edition: A Personal Guide to Turning from Alcoholism & Other Addictions—Drugs, Food, Gambling, Sex... *By Rabbi Kerry M. Olitzky and Stuart A. Copans, MD; Preface by Abraham J. Twerski, MD* 6 x 9, 160 pp, Quality PB, 978-1-58023-409-2 **$16.99**

Spirituality

Repentance: The Meaning and Practice of *Teshuvah*
By Dr. Louis E. Newman; Foreword by Rabbi Harold M. Schulweis; Preface by Rabbi Karyn D. Kedar
Examines both the practical and philosophical dimensions of *teshuvah*, Judaism's core religious-moral teaching on repentance, and its value for us—Jews and non-Jews alike—today. 6 x 9, 256 pp, HC, 978-1-58023-426-9 **$24.99**

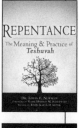

Tanya, the Masterpiece of Hasidic Wisdom
Selections Annotated & Explained
Translation & Annotation by Rabbi Rami Shapiro; Foreword by Rabbi Zalman M. Schachter-Shalomi
Brings the genius of *Tanya,* one of the most powerful books of Jewish wisdom, to anyone seeking to deepen their understanding of the soul.
5½ x 8½, 240 pp, Quality PB, 978-1-59473-275-1 **$16.99**
(A book from SkyLight Paths, Jewish Lights' sister imprint)

Aleph-Bet Yoga: Embodying the Hebrew Letters for Physical and Spiritual Well-Being
By Steven A. Rapp; Foreword by Tamar Frankiel, PhD, and Judy Greenfeld; Preface by Hart Lazer
7 x 10, 128 pp, b/w photos, Quality PB, Lay-flat binding, 978-1-58023-162-6 **$16.95**

A Book of Life: Embracing Judaism as a Spiritual Practice
By Rabbi Michael Strassfeld 6 x 9, 544 pp, Quality PB, 978-1-58023-247-0 **$19.99**

Bringing the Psalms to Life: How to Understand and Use the Book of Psalms
By Rabbi Daniel F. Polish, PhD 6 x 9, 208 pp, Quality PB, 978-1-58023-157-2 **$16.95**

Does the Soul Survive? A Jewish Journey to Belief in Afterlife, Past Lives & Living with Purpose *By Rabbi Elie Kaplan Spitz; Foreword by Brian L. Weiss, MD*
6 x 9, 288 pp, Quality PB, 978-1-58023-165-7 **$16.99**

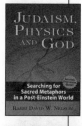

First Steps to a New Jewish Spirit: Reb Zalman's Guide to Recapturing the Intimacy & Ecstasy in Your Relationship with God *By Rabbi Zalman M. Schachter-Shalomi with Donald Gropman* 6 x 9, 144 pp, Quality PB, 978-1-58023-182-4 **$16.95**

Foundations of Sephardic Spirituality: The Inner Life of Jews of the Ottoman Empire
By Rabbi Marc D. Angel, PhD 6 x 9, 224 pp, Quality PB, 978-1-58023-341-5 **$18.99**

God & the Big Bang: Discovering Harmony between Science & Spirituality
By Dr. Daniel C. Matt 6 x 9, 216 pp, Quality PB, 978-1-879045-89-7 **$16.99**

God in Our Relationships: Spirituality between People from the Teachings of Martin Buber *By Rabbi Dennis S. Ross* 5½ x 8½, 160 pp, Quality PB, 978-1-58023-147-3 **$16.95**

The Jewish Lights Spirituality Handbook: A Guide to Understanding, Exploring & Living a Spiritual Life *Edited by Stuart M. Matlins*
What exactly is "Jewish" about spirituality? How do I make it a part of my life? Fifty of today's foremost spiritual leaders share their ideas and experience with us.
6 x 9, 456 pp, Quality PB, 978-1-58023-093-3 **$19.99**

Judaism, Physics and God: Searching for Sacred Metaphors in a Post-Einstein World
By Rabbi David W. Nelson 6 x 9, 352 pp, Quality PB, inc. reader's discussion guide,
978-1-58023-306-4 **$18.99**; HC, 352 pp, 978-1-58023-252-4 **$24.99**

Meaning & Mitzvah: Daily Practices for Reclaiming Judaism through Prayer, God, Torah, Hebrew, Mitzvot and Peoplehood *By Rabbi Goldie Milgram*
7 x 9, 336 pp, Quality PB, 978-1-58023-256-2 **$19.99**

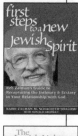

Minding the Temple of the Soul: Balancing Body, Mind, and Spirit through Traditional Jewish Prayer, Movement, and Meditation *By Tamar Frankiel, PhD, and Judy Greenfeld*
7 x 10, 184 pp, Illus., Quality PB, 978-1-879045-64-4 **$18.99**

One God Clapping: The Spiritual Path of a Zen Rabbi *By Rabbi Alan Lew with Sherril Jaffe*
5½ x 8½, 336 pp, Quality PB, 978-1-58023-115-2 **$16.95**

The Soul of the Story: Meetings with Remarkable People
By Rabbi David Zeller 6 x 9, 288 pp, HC, 978-1-58023-272-2 **$21.99**

There Is No Messiah ... and You're It: The Stunning Transformation of Judaism's Most Provocative Idea *By Rabbi Robert N. Levine, DD*
6 x 9, 192 pp, Quality PB, 978-1-58023-255-5 **$16.99**

These Are the Words: A Vocabulary of Jewish Spiritual Life
By Rabbi Arthur Green, PhD 6 x 9, 304 pp, Quality PB, 978-1-58023-107-7 **$18.95**

Holidays/Holy Days

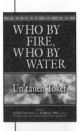

Who by Fire, Who by Water—Un'taneh Tokef
Edited by Rabbi Lawrence A. Hoffman, PhD
Examines the prayer's theology, authorship and poetry through a set of lively essays, all written in accessible language.
6 x 9, 272 pp, HC, 978-1-58023-424-5 **$24.99**

All These Vows—Kol Nidre
Edited by Rabbi Lawrence A. Hoffman, PhD
The most memorable prayer of the Jewish New Year—what it means, why we sing it, and the secret of its magical appeal.
6 x 9, 288 pp, HC, 978-1-58023-430-6 **$24.99**

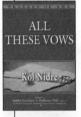

Rosh Hashanah Readings: Inspiration, Information and Contemplation
Yom Kippur Readings: Inspiration, Information and Contemplation
  Edited by Rabbi Dov Peretz Elkins; Section Introductions from Arthur Green's These Are the Words
  Rosh Hashanah: 6 x 9, 400 pp, Quality PB, 978-1-58023-437-5 **$19.99**; HC, 978-1-58023-239-5 **$24.99**
  Yom Kippur: 6 x 9, 368 pp, Quality PB, 978-1-58023-438-2 **$19.99**; HC, 978-1-58023-271-5 **$24.99**

Jewish Holidays: A Brief Introduction for Christians
By Rabbi Kerry M. Olitzky and Rabbi Daniel Judson
5½ x 8½, 176 pp, Quality PB, 978-1-58023-302-6 **$16.99**

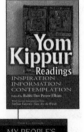

Reclaiming Judaism as a Spiritual Practice: Holy Days and Shabbat
By Rabbi Goldie Milgram 7 x 9, 272 pp, Quality PB, 978-1-58023-205-0 **$19.99**

Shabbat, 2nd Edition: The Family Guide to Preparing for and Celebrating the Sabbath
By Dr. Ron Wolfson 7 x 9, 320 pp, Illus., Quality PB, 978-1-58023-164-0 **$19.99**

Hanukkah, 2nd Edition: The Family Guide to Spiritual Celebration
By Dr. Ron Wolfson 7 x 9, 240 pp, Illus., Quality PB, 978-1-58023-122-0 **$18.95**

The Jewish Family Fun Book, 2nd Edition
Holiday Projects, Everyday Activities, and Travel Ideas with Jewish Themes
  By Danielle Dardashti and Roni Sarig; Illus. by Avi Katz
6 x 9, 304 pp, 70+ b/w illus. & diagrams, Quality PB, 978-1-58023-333-0 **$18.99**

Passover

My People's Passover Haggadah
Traditional Texts, Modern Commentaries
Edited by Rabbi Lawrence A. Hoffman, PhD, and David Arnow, PhD
A diverse and exciting collection of commentaries on the traditional Passover Haggadah—in two volumes!
Vol. 1: 7 x 10, 304 pp, HC, 978-1-58023-354-5 **$24.99**
Vol. 2: 7 x 10, 320 pp, HC, 978-1-58023-346-0 **$24.99**

Freedom Journeys: The Tale of Exodus and Wilderness across Millennia
By Rabbi Arthur O. Waskow and Rabbi Phyllis O. Berman
Explores how the story of Exodus echoes in our own time, calling us to relearn and rethink the Passover story through social-justice, ecological, feminist and interfaith perspectives. 6 x 9, 288 pp, HC, 978-1-58023-445-0 **$24.99**

Leading the Passover Journey: The Seder's Meaning Revealed,
the Haggadah's Story Retold By Rabbi Nathan Laufer
Uncovers the hidden meaning of the Seder's rituals and customs.
6 x 9, 224 pp, Quality PB, 978-1-58023-399-6 **$18.99**; HC, 978-1-58023-211-1 **$24.99**

Creating Lively Passover Seders, 2nd Edition: A Sourcebook of Engaging Tales,
Texts & Activities By David Arnow, PhD 7 x 9, 464 pp, Quality PB, 978-1-58023-444-3 **$24.99**

Passover, 2nd Edition: The Family Guide to Spiritual Celebration
By Dr. Ron Wolfson with Joel Lurie Grishaver 7 x 9, 416 pp, Quality PB, 978-1-58023-174-9 **$19.95**

The Women's Passover Companion: Women's Reflections on the Festival of Freedom
Edited by Rabbi Sharon Cohen Anisfeld, Tara Mohr and Catherine Spector; Foreword by Paula E. Hyman
6 x 9, 352 pp, Quality PB, 978-1-58023-231-9 **$19.99**; HC, 978-1-58023-128-2 **$24.95**

The Women's Seder Sourcebook: Rituals & Readings for Use at the Passover Seder
Edited by Rabbi Sharon Cohen Anisfeld, Tara Mohr and Catherine Spector
6 x 9, 384 pp, Quality PB, 978-1-58023-232-6 **$19.99**

Life Cycle

Marriage/Parenting/Family/Aging

The New Jewish Baby Album: Creating and Celebrating the Beginning of a Spiritual Life—A Jewish Lights Companion
By the Editors at Jewish Lights; Foreword by Anita Diamant; Preface by Rabbi Sandy Eisenberg Sasso
A spiritual keepsake that will be treasured for generations. More than just a memory book, *shows you how—and why it's important*—to create a Jewish home and a Jewish life. 8 x 10, 64 pp, Deluxe Padded HC, Full-color illus., 978-1-58023-138-1 **$19.95**

The Jewish Pregnancy Book: A Resource for the Soul, Body & Mind during Pregnancy, Birth & the First Three Months *By Sandy Falk, MD, and Rabbi Daniel Judson, with Steven A. Rapp* Medical information, prayers and rituals for each stage of pregnancy. 7 x 10, 208 pp, b/w photos, Quality PB, 978-1-58023-178-7 **$16.95**

Celebrating Your New Jewish Daughter: Creating Jewish Ways to Welcome Baby Girls into the Covenant—New and Traditional Ceremonies *By Debra Nussbaum Cohen; Foreword by Rabbi Sandy Eisenberg Sasso* 6 x 9, 272 pp, Quality PB, 978-1-58023-090-2 **$18.95**

The New Jewish Baby Book, 2nd Edition: Names, Ceremonies & Customs—A Guide for Today's Families *By Anita Diamant* 6 x 9, 320 pp, Quality PB, 978-1-58023-251-7 **$19.99**

Parenting as a Spiritual Journey: Deepening Ordinary and Extraordinary Events into Sacred Occasions *By Rabbi Nancy Fuchs-Kreimer, PhD*
6 x 9, 224 pp, Quality PB, 978-1-58023-016-2 **$17.99**

Parenting Jewish Teens: A Guide for the Perplexed
By Joanne Doades Explores the questions and issues that shape the world in which today's Jewish teenagers live and offers constructive advice to parents.
6 x 9, 176 pp, Quality PB, 978-1-58023-305-7 **$16.99**

Judaism for Two: A Spiritual Guide for Strengthening and Celebrating Your Loving Relationship *By Rabbi Nancy Fuchs-Kreimer, PhD, and Rabbi Nancy H. Wiener, DMin; Foreword by Rabbi Elliot N. Dorff, PhD*
Addresses the ways Jewish teachings can enhance and strengthen committed relationships. 6 x 9, 224 pp, Quality PB, 978-1-58023-254-8 **$16.99**

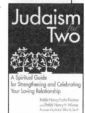

The Creative Jewish Wedding Book, 2nd Edition: A Hands-On Guide to New & Old Traditions, Ceremonies & Celebrations *By Gabrielle Kaplan-Mayer*
9 x 9, 288 pp, b/w photos, Quality PB, 978-1-58023-398-9 **$19.99**

Divorce Is a Mitzvah: A Practical Guide to Finding Wholeness and Holiness When Your Marriage Dies *By Rabbi Perry Netter; Afterword by Rabbi Laura Geller*
6 x 9, 224 pp, Quality PB, 978-1-58023-172-5 **$16.95**

Embracing the Covenant: Converts to Judaism Talk About Why & How
By Rabbi Allan Berkowitz and Patti Moskovitz 6 x 9, 192 pp, Quality PB, 978-1-879045-50-7 **$16.95**

The Guide to Jewish Interfaith Family Life: An InterfaithFamily.com Handbook
Edited by Ronnie Friedland and Edmund Case
6 x 9, 384 pp, Quality PB, 978-1-58023-153-4 **$18.95**

A Heart of Wisdom: Making the Jewish Journey from Midlife through the Elder Years
Edited by Susan Berrin; Foreword by Rabbi Harold Kushner
6 x 9, 384 pp, Quality PB, 978-1-58023-051-3 **$18.95**

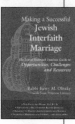

Introducing My Faith and My Community: The Jewish Outreach Institute Guide for the Christian in a Jewish Interfaith Relationship
By Rabbi Kerry M. Olitzky 6 x 9, 176 pp, Quality PB, 978-1-58023-192-3 **$16.99**

Making a Successful Jewish Interfaith Marriage: The Jewish Outreach Institute Guide to Opportunities, Challenges and Resources *By Rabbi Kerry M. Olitzky with Joan Peterson Littman*
6 x 9, 176 pp, Quality PB, 978-1-58023-170-1 **$16.95**

A Man's Responsibility: A Jewish Guide to Being a Son, a Partner in Marriage, a Father and a Community Leader *By Rabbi Joseph B. Meszler*
6 x 9, 192 pp, Quality PB, 978-1-58023-435-1 **$16.99**; HC, 978-1-58023-362-0 **$21.99**

So That Your Values Live On: Ethical Wills and How to Prepare Them
Edited by Rabbi Jack Riemer and Rabbi Nathaniel Stampfer
6 x 9, 272 pp, Quality PB, 978-1-879045-34-7 **$18.99**

Inspiration

God of Me: Imagining God throughout Your Lifetime
By Rabbi David Lyon Helps you cut through preconceived ideas of God and dogmas that stifle your creativity when thinking about your personal relationship with God. 6 x 9, 176 pp, Quality PB, 978-1-58023-452-8 **$16.99**

The God Upgrade: Finding Your 21st-Century Spirituality in Judaism's 5,000-Year-Old Tradition *By Rabbi Jamie Korngold; Foreword by Rabbi Harold M. Schulweis* A provocative look at how our changing God concepts have shaped every aspect of Judaism. 6 x 9, 176 pp, Quality PB, 978-1-58023-443-3 **$15.99**

The Seven Questions You're Asked in Heaven: Reviewing and Renewing Your Life on Earth *By Dr. Ron Wolfson* An intriguing and entertaining resource for living a life that matters. 6 x 9, 176 pp, Quality PB, 978-1-58023-407-8 **$16.99**

Happiness and the Human Spirit: The Spirituality of Becoming the Best You Can Be *By Rabbi Abraham J. Twerski, MD* Shows you that true happiness is attainable once you stop looking outside yourself for the source. 6 x 9, 176 pp, Quality PB, 978-1-58023-404-7 **$16.99**; HC, 978-1-58023-343-9 **$19.99**

A Formula for Proper Living: Practical Lessons from Life and Torah
By Rabbi Abraham J. Twerski, MD 6 x 9, 144 pp, HC, 978-1-58023-402-3 **$19.99**

The Bridge to Forgiveness: Stories and Prayers for Finding God and Restoring Wholeness *By Rabbi Karyn D. Kedar* 6 x 9, 176 pp, Quality PB, 978-1-58023-451-1 **$16.99**

The Empty Chair: Finding Hope and Joy—Timeless Wisdom from a Hasidic Master, Rebbe Nachman of Breslov *Adapted by Moshe Mykoff and the Breslov Research Institute* 4 x 6, 128 pp, Deluxe PB w/ flaps, 978-1-879045-67-5 **$9.99**

The Gentle Weapon: Prayers for Everyday and Not-So-Everyday Moments—Timeless Wisdom from the Teachings of the Hasidic Master, Rebbe Nachman of Breslov *Adapted by Moshe Mykoff and S. C. Mizrahi, together with the Breslov Research Institute* 4 x 6, 144 pp, Deluxe PB w/ flaps, 978-1-58023-022-3 **$9.99**

God Whispers: Stories of the Soul, Lessons of the Heart *By Rabbi Karyn D. Kedar* 6 x 9, 176 pp, Quality PB, 978-1-58023-088-9 **$15.95**

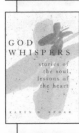

God's To-Do List: 103 Ways to Be an Angel and Do God's Work on Earth
By Dr. Ron Wolfson 6 x 9, 144 pp, Quality PB, 978-1-58023-301-9 **$16.99**

Jewish Stories from Heaven and Earth: Inspiring Tales to Nourish the Heart and Soul *Edited by Rabbi Dov Peretz Elkins* 6 x 9, 304 pp, Quality PB, 978-1-58023-363-7 **$16.99**

Life's Daily Blessings: Inspiring Reflections on Gratitude and Joy for Every Day, Based on Jewish Wisdom *By Rabbi Kerry M. Olitzky* 4½ x 6½, 368 pp, Quality PB, 978-1-58023-396-5 **$16.99**

Restful Reflections: Nighttime Inspiration to Calm the Soul, Based on Jewish Wisdom *By Rabbi Kerry M. Olitzky and Rabbi Lori Forman* 4½ x 6½, 448 pp, Quality PB, 978-1-58023-091-9 **$15.95**

Sacred Intentions: Morning Inspiration to Strengthen the Spirit, Based on Jewish Wisdom *By Rabbi Kerry M. Olitzky and Rabbi Lori Forman* 4½ x 6½, 448 pp, Quality PB, 978-1-58023-061-2 **$16.99**

Kabbalah/Mysticism

Jewish Mysticism and the Spiritual Life: Classical Texts, Contemporary Reflections *Edited by Dr. Lawrence Fine, Dr. Eitan Fishbane and Rabbi Or N. Rose* Inspirational and thought-provoking materials for contemplation, discussion and action. 6 x 9, 256 pp, HC, 978-1-58023-434-4 **$24.99**

Ehyeh: A Kabbalah for Tomorrow
By Rabbi Arthur Green, PhD 6 x 9, 224 pp, Quality PB, 978-1-58023-213-5 **$18.99**

The Gift of Kabbalah: Discovering the Secrets of Heaven, Renewing Your Life on Earth *By Tamar Frankiel, PhD* 6 x 9, 256 pp, Quality PB, 978-1-58023-141-1 **$16.95**

Seek My Face: A Jewish Mystical Theology *By Rabbi Arthur Green, PhD*
6 x 9, 304 pp, Quality PB, 978-1-58023-130-5 **$19.95**

Zohar: Annotated & Explained *Translation & Annotation by Dr. Daniel C. Matt; Foreword by Andrew Harvey* 5½ x 8½, 176 pp, Quality PB, 978-1-893361-51-5 **$15.99**
(A book from SkyLight Paths, Jewish Lights' sister imprint)

See also *The Way Into Jewish Mystical Tradition* in The Way Into... Series.

Children's Books by Sandy Eisenberg Sasso

Adam & Eve's First Sunset: God's New Day
Explores fear and hope, faith and gratitude in ways that will delight kids and adults—inspiring us to bless each of God's days and nights.
9 x 12, 32 pp, Full-color illus., HC, 978-1-58023-177-0 **$17.95** *For ages 4 & up*

Also Available as a Board Book: **Adam and Eve's New Day**
5 x 5, 24 pp, Full-color illus., Board Book, 978-1-59473-205-8 **$7.99** *For ages 0–4*
(A book from SkyLight Paths, Jewish Lights' sister imprint)

But God Remembered: Stories of Women from Creation to the Promised Land
Four different stories of women—Lilith, Serach, Bityah and the Daughters of Z—teach us important values through their faith and actions.
9 x 12, 32 pp, Full-color illus., Quality PB, 978-1-58023-372-9 **$8.99** *For ages 8 & up*

Cain & Abel: Finding the Fruits of Peace
Shows children that we have the power to deal with anger in positive ways. Provides questions for kids and adults to explore together.
9 x 12, 32 pp, Full-color illus., HC, 978-1-58023-123-7 **$16.95** *For ages 5 & up*

For Heaven's Sake
Heaven is often found where you least expect it.
9 x 12, 32 pp, Full-color illus., HC, 978-1-58023-054-4 **$16.95** *For ages 4 & up*

God in Between
If you wanted to find God, where would you look? This magical, mythical tale teaches that God can be found where we are: within all of us and the relationships between us. 9 x 12, 32 pp, Full-color illus., HC, 978-1-879045-86-6 **$16.95** *For ages 4 & up*

God Said Amen
An inspiring story about hearing the answers to our prayers.
9 x 12, 32 pp, Full-color illus., HC, 978-1-58023-080-3 **$16.95** *For ages 4 & up*

God's Paintbrush: Special 10th Anniversary Edition
Wonderfully interactive, invites children of all faiths and backgrounds to encounter God through moments in their own lives. Provides questions adult and child can explore together. 11 x 8½, 32 pp, Full-color illus., HC, 978-1-58023-195-4 **$17.95** *For ages 4 & up*

Also Available as a Board Book: **I Am God's Paintbrush**
5 x 5, 24 pp, Full-color illus., Board Book, 978-1-59473-265-2 **$7.99** *For ages 0–4*
(A book from SkyLight Paths, Jewish Lights' sister imprint)

Also Available: **God's Paintbrush Teacher's Guide**
8½ x 11, 32 pp, PB, 978-1-879045-57-6 **$8.95**

God's Paintbrush Celebration Kit
A Spiritual Activity Kit for Teachers and Students of All Faiths, All Backgrounds
9½ x 12, 40 Full-color Activity Sheets & Teacher Folder w/ complete instructions
HC, 978-1-58023-050-6 **$21.95**
8-Student Activity Sheet Pack (40 sheets/5 sessions), 978-1-58023-058-2 **$19.95**

In God's Name
Like an ancient myth in its poetic text and vibrant illustrations, this award-winning modern fable about the search for God's name celebrates the diversity and, at the same time, the unity of all people.
9 x 12, 32 pp, Full-color illus., HC, 978-1-879045-26-2 **$16.99** *For ages 4 & up*

Also Available as a Board Book: **What Is God's Name?**
5 x 5, 24 pp, Full-color illus., Board Book, 978-1-893361-10-2 **$7.99** *For ages 0–4*
(A book from SkyLight Paths, Jewish Lights' sister imprint)

Also Available in Spanish: **El nombre de Dios**
9 x 12, 32 pp, Full-color illus., HC, 978-1-893361-63-8 **$16.95** *For ages 4 & up*

Noah's Wife: The Story of Naamah
When God tells Noah to bring the animals of the world onto the ark, God also calls on Naamah, Noah's wife, to save each plant on Earth. Based on an ancient text.
9 x 12, 32 pp, Full-color illus., HC, 978-1-58023-134-3 **$16.95** *For ages 4 & up*

Also Available as a Board Book: **Naamah, Noah's Wife**
5 x 5, 24 pp, Full-color illus., Board Book, 978-1-893361-56-0 **$7.95** *For ages 0–4*
(A book from SkyLight Paths, Jewish Lights' sister imprint)

Congregation Resources

Empowered Judaism: What Independent Minyanim Can Teach Us about Building Vibrant Jewish Communities
By Rabbi Elie Kaunfer; Foreword by Prof. Jonathan D. Sarna
Examines the independent minyan movement and the lessons these grassroots communities can provide. 6 x 9, 224 pp, Quality PB, 978-1-58023-412-2 **$18.99**

Spiritual Boredom: Rediscovering the Wonder of Judaism *By Dr. Erica Brown*
Breaks through the surface of spiritual boredom to find the reservoir of meaning within. 6 x 9, 208 pp, HC, 978-1-58023-405-4 **$21.99**

Building a Successful Volunteer Culture
Finding Meaning in Service in the Jewish Community
By Rabbi Charles Simon; Foreword by Shelley Lindauer; Preface by Dr. Ron Wolfson
Shows you how to develop and maintain the volunteers who are essential to the vitality of your organization and community. 6 x 9, 192 pp, Quality PB, 978-1-58023-408-5 **$16.99**

The Case for Jewish Peoplehood: Can We Be One?
By Dr. Erica Brown and Dr. Misha Galperin; Foreword by Rabbi Joseph Telushkin
6 x 9, 224 pp, HC, 978-1-58023-401-6 **$21.99**

Inspired Jewish Leadership: Practical Approaches to Building Strong Communities
By Dr. Erica Brown 6 x 9, 256 pp, HC, 978-1-58023-361-3 **$24.99**

Jewish Pastoral Care, 2nd Edition: A Practical Handbook from Traditional & Contemporary Sources *Edited by Rabbi Dayle A. Friedman, MSW, MAJCS, BCC*
6 x 9, 528 pp, Quality PB, 978-1-58023-427-6 **$30.00**

Rethinking Synagogues: A New Vocabulary for Congregational Life
By Rabbi Lawrence A. Hoffman, PhD 6 x 9, 240 pp, Quality PB, 978-1-58023-248-7 **$19.99**

The Spirituality of Welcoming: How to Transform Your Congregation into a Sacred Community *By Dr. Ron Wolfson* 6 x 9, 224 pp, Quality PB, 978-1-58023-244-9 **$19.99**

Children's Books

Around the World in One Shabbat
Jewish People Celebrate the Sabbath Together
By Durga Yael Bernhard

Takes your child on a colorful adventure to share the many ways Jewish people celebrate Shabbat around the world.
11 x 8½, 32 pp, Full-color illus. HC, 978-1-58023-433-7 **$18.99** *For ages 3–6*

What You Will See Inside a Synagogue
By Rabbi Lawrence A. Hoffman, PhD, and Dr. Ron Wolfson; Full-color photos by Bill Aron
A colorful, fun-to-read introduction that explains the ways and whys of Jewish worship and religious life.
8½ x 10½, 32 pp, Full-color photos, Quality PB, 978-1-59473-256-0 **$8.99** *For ages 6 & up*
(A book from SkyLight Paths, Jewish Lights' sister imprint)

Because Nothing Looks Like God
By Lawrence Kushner and Karen Kushner Introduces children to the possibilities of spiritual life. 11 x 8½, 32 pp, Full-color illus., HC, 978-1-58023-092-6 **$17.99** *For ages 4 & up*

The Book of Miracles: A Young Person's Guide to Jewish Spiritual Awareness
Written and illus. by Lawrence Kushner
6 x 9, 96 pp, 2-color illus., HC, 978-1-879045-78-1 **$16.95** *For ages 9–13*

In God's Hands *By Lawrence Kushner and Gary Schmidt* 9 x 12, 32 pp, Full-color illus., HC, 978-1-58023-224-1 **$16.99** *For ages 5 & up*

In Our Image: God's First Creatures *By Nancy Sohn Swartz*
9 x 12, 32 pp, Full-color illus., HC, 978-1-879045-99-6 **$16.95** *For ages 4 & up*

The Kids' Fun Book of Jewish Time
By Emily Sper 9 x 7½, 24 pp, Full-color illus., HC, 978-1-58023-311-8 **$16.99** *For ages 3–6*

What Makes Someone a Jew? *By Lauren Seidman*
Reflects the changing face of American Judaism.
10 x 8½, 32 pp, Full-color photos, Quality PB, 978-1-58023-321-7 **$8.99** *For ages 3–6*